Among the Pages

Davena Buck

PublishAmerica
Baltimore

ISBN: 1-4241-5529-0
PUBLISHED BY PUBLISHAMERICA, LLLP
www.publishamerica.com
Baltimore

Printed in the United States of America

I would like to dedicate this book to Verna Buck.

Acknowledgments

I would like to thank my family for listening to my constant chatter about this book. My son Greg, who is my computer whiz, and son Chad, who walked me through a man's thinking, daughter Brenda, who was there when things overwhelmed me, and my other daughter Niki, who always smiles and says you can do this Mom. A special thanks to my daughter-in-law Kimberly, who read and worked through the chapters with me. I would also like to thank a very special friend, who knows who they are, for believing in me and giving me the courage and the push to write this. And last, but not least, a special thanks to my husband John, who didn't seem to mind my late night get-ups to write at three in the morning and still kept his smile and a great sense of humor.

Sometimes our lives take a turn and it does not seem to matter what was before or what will be thereafter, and if we could have had control, it might make it for the worse...and yet we live our lives from day to day. Once in awhile fate comes knockin' at our door, and we are helpless to change things. We think from our childhood that we have the world by the tail and that no matter what we do, can or will affect us, but sometimes, yes, sometimes we don't have the control over the events in our lives, how we feel...*or*...who we love...

Chapter One

She could hear the old pickup truck as it meandered and whined its way down the dirt road. It had a certain sound that only belonged to it, as it coughed and wheezed. She had teased Richard many times about fixing the pang in it, and he would just laugh and say, "One of these days when the old girl gives up, I'll buy me a new one." Her heartbeat began to quicken and her breathing halted as she realized he was not that far from her place. Looking in the mirror, with her fingertips she brushed the hair from her face as she listened to the approaching truck. She felt her hands shake with excitement as the sound grew closer. Bess wasn't a very tall woman, and her eyes were a striking blue that jumped out at you when she smiled. She had lived on the place for three years, ever since her dad had suddenly died of a heart attack and left it to her. He only had a few head of cows, a five year old mare, a stud named Teco, some chickens, an old tomcat named Jack and a dog named Rocky. Her father's death was sudden and it left a lot of unanswered questions that Bess was not sure she would ever know the answers to. Like the locket he left behind, it had a picture of her mom and a baby in it, but it didn't look like the other baby pictures she had of herself and him. This left her wondering. The small ranch she had learned to call home consisted of forty acres of real prime land that lay down in a small valley just south of the town called Lakeview. It bordered on a creek that gave it a natural green in the summertime and provided water to God's creatures large and small alike. The house was not a big one and it could do with some paint, but when the flowers bloomed in the summertime you only saw the colors they brought to the old house. She had worked in the city before her dad's death, in a greenhouse. It was the closest thing she could get to being near the ranch without actually going home, and it gave her the feeling of being in tune with the earth. She loved the outdoors and her friends often remarked she had the Midas touch, only instead of gold everything turned green. But now the snow was on the ground, and spring a ways to come and the sound of a truck was not far off.

Bess hollered at the dog as he scrambled out the door nearly knocking her down, for he recognized the sound of that truck too. The wind had come up and Bess threw her jacket on to keep the biting cold from seeping in. She marveled every time at the old barn, wondering how it stood up to the weather and time itself. It was beyond repair, and she was well aware of the fact she was in desperate need of a new one. But like all things, unless you were made of money, it was the in need of that came first and not the in want of. Bess walked out, heading for the barn in hopes that Richard would see her, expecting she was headed out there with things to do. Heaven forbid he should know how she really felt.

Richard was a tall man with a slender build, his broad strong shoulders set off his body making his muscles stand out. His receding hairline was attractive as was the mustache he possessed. His hair, the color of winter wheat with a touch of red and eyes a baby blue. He sported a few lines on his face, but all in all he was a handsome man for the age of fifty and God had been kind to him.

"Come on, Rocky," Bess hollered as the dog slipped in step with her.

The truck came to a slow grinding halt as it pulled into her driveway. She smiled secretly to herself as she waved to him.

"Hey, how you been?" he said, smiling

"I'm okay, and you?" She thought to herself, *He sure is easy on the eyes.*

"Oh, the same, I guess. The reason I stopped by was to see if you needed anything from town. I'm heading in to get feed for the chickens and I remembered you mentioned you were low."

"Well, as a matter of fact, I am," she said. "Want some coffee before you go? I just made a fresh pot."

"Thanks, that sounds real good," he said, rubbing his cold hands together. "You sure have made this place look real cozy. I remember what it looked like when your dad was alive. Ahhhh…no offence intended," he said, smiling as he stepped through the door.

"And none taken," said Bess. "Thanks, I like to dabble with arts and crafts, it helps to pass the winter by."

"You should have been a rancher's wife." He smiled, his eyes drinking in everything he saw.

With this she blushed, watching his every move.

"Say, how about you stay for supper when you get back. I have a couple chickens in the pot, and you won't have to go home to a cold house and a cold supper?"

"I wish I could," he said dreamily, "but the kids are supposed to call and I need to be there to answer."

"I understand," said Bess. "Maybe some other time you and the kids can come to a Sunday dinner."

"Yeah," he said, "that would be nice real nice."

"When are the kids coming back?"

"I'm not real sure right now. Mary's folk want to spend some time with them. It's been real tough for them with Mary gone. It's the not knowing where she is, that's the hard part. She's the only one they have, ahhh, daughter, you know. Anyway," he said, his mind went adrift for a moment. Then as he rose up from the table, he looked at her, his eyes smiling. "Thanks for the coffee there, kiddo, it was good. Say, did you tell me you wanted two sacks of feed?"

Bess smiled. "I didn't say, but yes that would be fine. Could you pick me up a sack of flour too? Say twenty-five pounds?" She followed him out the door and to his pickup handing him her money.

"Sure, anything for you, smiley." He grinned, stuffing it into his pocket. His eyes glazed over for a moment and he looked as if he started to say something to her, only to shut his door and turn the key. "See you later," he said.

She waved goodbye as she watched him drive off in his truck. She caught her breath. Her mind drifted along the road with him until she could no longer see him in sight.

"Come on," she hollered to Rocky, "its cold out here," and just as the door was about to close Jack slipped inside, purring as he rubbed alongside of the dog.

Chapter Two

The wind picked up, whistling cold in through the cracks of the door, sending a slight chill and shiver down Bess's back. She knew it wouldn't be long before another storm would arrive, and in this country you needed to always be prepared. With that thought in mind she opened the stove and tossed in another piece of wood.

"Well, boys," she said, talking to the two curled up by the stove, "I have to go back out to the barn and feed all the children out there? Any takers? I thought not," she said, smiling; "I noticed how you both just jumped right up to help me, real helpful you are. The both of you!"

She laughed as she put on her heavy coat and hat, reaching into her pocket she felt her gloves and was glad she had picked up an extra pair when she had been in town last.

The door flew open when she turned the handle, banging against the wall as it slipped from her hand. The wind had picked up and snow was beginning to fall in just the small amount of time she had been indoors.

Bess locked down the chickens, making sure they had enough water and the light was on. She rolled up a couple hundred feet of rope that had been laying off to the side and decided to take it to the storeroom off the front porch where she kept some of her tack.

The barn rattled against the wind, but even as old as it was, it held its own. The light was starting to fade, and fast. Bess knew she had to pick up the pace or light up the lantern that was hanging on the pole inside the barn next to her window. Climbing up the ladder, she threw down several bales of hay, enough to last so she wouldn't have to go up in the morning. Each of her two horses got a flake and a small can of oats. This was the time of day she really liked as she reached over to touch each of her horses. After filling their water trough, she filled the one just outside the gate for the cows. When everyone was taken care of, she switched on the outside light and headed back to the house. It was getting colder, and a chill went up her back. She hugged herself, rubbing her arms to get warm. "Yep, it's going to storm any minute," she said.

Chapter Three

Bess rechecked all the windows, making sure everything was buttoned down tight. She had forgotten to close the one in the kitchen; it was still open a crack from breakfast that morning.

"Dang," she said as she pulled and tugged at the window. Looking out, she saw swirls of snow coming down. "It must have swelled with the damp and cold." Bess pulled with all she had and it just wouldn't budge. "Maybe when our friend gets back with the feed he'll close it for us, that is if he decides to still come our way," she said with a dreamy look in her eyes.

The old dog nudged her pants leg as if to say he understood everything she had to say. Bess reached down and touched his head gently, and said, "Come on, ol' boy, let's go upstairs and get the lanterns. I have a feeling we will be without electricity before the night is through." At that moment the lights flickered as if in reply to her words.

She reached the upstairs and pulled the ladder down and began climbing up into the attic. She hadn't been up there much since her father had passed away, so boxes and more boxes were stacked. There were many she had not gone through. They were left for another day. Looking out the small window Bess realized the light was almost gone. She took note that the snow was coming down in more than a flurry now and the wind sounded bitter and cold.

"I wonder what's taking Richard so long?" she said aloud, wearing a frown on her face. She was worried. "Maybe he went on home with this storm brewing." She sighed. "Anyway, I need to get these lanterns downstairs and pronto." Two of them needed filling and so she hung the full one above the kitchen sink window, making sure she had matches nearby.

Bess sat down rubbing her neck; it was getting late, and she suddenly felt very tired. She reached over and touched the dog gently. Her voice was soft and quiet. "Sometimes, Rocky, life can be very lonely."

Just then the phone began ringing. By the fourth ring she had picked it up. "Hello?"

"Hi, Bess, this is Jake. Say, you haven't seen Rich, have you? He'd mentioned he might stop by."

"No, not since early this afternoon, said he was headed for town, and was stopping by the feed store, and asked if I needed anything. I told him I could use some chicken feed and some flour, but I haven't seen him since. Thought he might have headed back to his place, what with this storm picking up speed like it is."

"Well," said Jake, "I didn't mean to bother you, it's just that this storm is worse, and I figured him to be home a long time ago. It looks like about six inches out there now, and it doesn't look to be letting up any time soon."

"I've been watching it through my windows and it's looking real bad, Jake, one of the worst we've seen in years. I don't know what to say about Richard though. Do you want me to have him give you a call if he decides to come this way anyway?"

"I sure would appreciate that, Bess," said Jake. "By the way, how are you doin' in the storm? You okay?"

"Well, yes. Thanks for askin', my lights have been flickering on and off all this afternoon. But I've got plenty of wood on the porch, and I cook with gas, so if the electricity goes out I'll be okay there. I have plenty water in the pantry, I just got the lanterns down from the attic and they're filled and ready to go. So...I'm looking pretty good," she said.

"Sounds like you have everything under control," said Jake. "All you need is a couple of chickens in a pot on the stove and you'd be all right."

Bess started laughing. "You are not going to believe this, but I have that covered too. I put a couple of such animals in the oven earlier today. I was making a dish for Sunday church."

"Sounds good to me." Jake laughed. "Good enough to come through this storm and invite myself to a set down."

"You're welcome anytime, Jake. There's more than enough."

"I'll take a rain check on that, hon, when the weather is a mite better and not so damn cold, excuse my French."

"No offense taken," said Bess

"Thanks," he said. "Just have him give me a jingle if you would, that's if he comes your way. Okay?"

"Sure will," she said. "See you later."

"Bye and thanks again," said Jake as he hung up the phone.

Chapter Four

Snow had been coming down at a steady pace. No one could remember when they had seen a storm of this size. The trucks, county and state alike, could not keep the snow off the roads. To make matters worse the wind was blowing fifty-five miles an hour causing drifts of four to five feet everywhere. It was not a night for anyone to be out, not man nor beast. The stores downtown closed their doors early and sent their employee's home hoping that they would beat the storm. Word was out it was not expected to let up for three days. An arctic front had blown in from Canada, down Washington and Montana on into Oregon. Roads where closed up and down the I-5. Hospitals were full, and emergency generators were going; electricity had been knock out by a downed power line. Word was they had heard an eighteen-wheeler had turned over. It had lost sight of the road on Highway 140 and gone into the ditch. The sheriff's office was on standby. They pulled in every available man and women. Telephones were out in some areas, and the electrical crews were working overtime. Visibility was zero; it was not a night to be out.

The Double A Café was open though, and the hospitality was, as always, of warmth and friendship. Ed and Irene had built their place from the bottom up. They ran everything on gas and kept a generator for the "just in cases" as Ed called them. Irene kept the coffee pots full and Ed rounded up candles and lanterns so that if the generators decided to fail they would be well prepared. They knew that it was important for the town that they were open, some place for everyone to go for coffee and a meal on a night like this. He had decided to keep the place open until the danger of this storm had passed. They would rotate the employees to make sure no one got over tired and personally see to it their getting to home and back again. For the workers' part in this, they would be amply rewarded with a big bonus.

The place was as full as its walls and seating could handle, and the noise level was at a roar, with laughter and voices and the clatter of dishes being served and cleared. New customers were coming in at a steady rate between work crews, State, County and City Police, and the travelers lost out in the storm.

As they finished getting warm and their bellies full, Ed did the thing he was so very good at, public relations. He called all the motels, and while most were booked he found lodging for the wayward and tired travelers. When these filled up, and there was not a single room to be had, Ed pulled in favors owed to him and found lodging for these folks with his customers in their homes. The stranded visitors were grateful for their kind generosity.

Irene ran a tight ship and kept everything going so smoothly, not only in the kitchen, but out on the floor. Everyone was a neighbor and a friend to them and the storm raged on.

Chapter Five

The sheriff's office was abuzz; phones ringing, radio operators chattering, officers handling large volumes of paperwork. Dispatch was working overtime; there was a flood of accident reports, missing people, and they had heard that someone had run into one of the storefront windows downtown. The sheriff had been in close contact with Ron, the city's police chief, and he knew that his hands were just as full. People were stuck and had slid off the road everywhere, power lines were down, and someone had broken into the liquor store.

All this and more were on high priority for Sheriff Baldwin and his comrades and demanded their full attention. The snowstorm had brought him a royal nightmare and he knew it had only just begun. The State and County snowplows were having a difficult time keeping up with the pace of the storm. This caused his office to work overtime keeping up with the overload of accidents caused by the storm. He wished people would just plain stay at home. But he knew from the past experience the storm only seemed to encourage them, and brought them out more, causing more accidents and problems. He called it their perpetual curiosity, and it got them into trouble every time, and him WELL overworked. He was wanted on the phone every five minutes, and he was getting irritated.

Finally he picked up the phone and punched into Bob's line and informed him to hold all calls unless it was life or death. He needed a mental break.

"I'm behind on my paperwork, Bob, and I have to finish up. Please," he said, "I need peace and quiet for a few minutes." He sat in his office with his door closed and put his head down, rubbing his forehead with his hands, and thought, *Why am I doing all this? I have more than enough money; I own property all over town that my uncle left me, so what is it about all this that I cannot resist? Well,* he thought, *I would be bored for one thing, I seem to need the excitement and the adrenalin rush and I like the power of this job. Yes, I really like having the adrenalin rush and power. Hummmmmm,* just when he felt himself relax a bit, BANG went the door.

In popped Officer Bob's head. "I know," he said, all drawn out, "you said you didn't want to be disturbed, but it's Jake Crammer, the foreman at the Gannon Ranch, and he insists he needs to talk to you."

"Okay," sighed Jeff, "I'll talk to him, put him on."

"He's on line three," said Bob.

"Before I pick this up," said Jeff, "did he happen to mention what this was all about?"

"Yup, said he was missing something."

"Okay. Put him through."

"Jake," he said as he punched open the line, "what can I do you for?"

"Well, Jeff, it's like this. I don't want sound like I'm jumpin' the gun, but you yourself know what this weather is like out there. Rich left this place hours ago. I called the feed store and Sally said he was in around four o'clock this afternoon. Picked up four sacks of chicken feed, two were for our neighbor Bess. He hasn't been seen since. No one at the café has seen him. I tried a few of the stores, and some of them were closed because of the storm. I'm fit to be tied, I just don't know where he could be. It's getting late, and he should have been here by now."

"Now I wouldn't go worrying about him just yet, Jake. He could be held up anywhere in this storm. Hell, look outside, I don't think anything is moving right at this moment. Besides, it's too soon to get your whiskers worked up over this. No one has reported seeing his rig anywhere; not my men, city police, or the road crews. My guess is he's holed up somewhere until this storm is over. And we won't find out about it until this is done."

"Well, I'm worried," said Jake. "It isn't like him to just disappear and not say a word."

"You're reading too much into this, Jake. You're worrying too much there, buddy. Besides, there isn't enough manpower available to start a rescue. He could be held up anywhere in this storm. I'll tell you what, let me put it this put it this way. If I don't hear from you, I will assume he made it back okay. Is that a deal?"

"Yeah, sure," said Jake. "He probably is holed up somewhere. Thanks anyway."

Jeff felt a little tug of worry, but he had too much to deal with to let it interfere. He decided he should call Sarah and take her back to his place. *Yes,* he thought, *that's exactly what I'm going to do. I'll deal with all this better if I just kick back a bit and relax,* and that's what he did He picked up the phone and dialed.

"Bob," he said standing next to his desk, "I'm heading home for a few. If you need me don't hesitate to call. Otherwise I'll be back in a couple of hours."

"Sure thing," said Bob. "Don't get snowed under."

"HA, you're real funny," said Jeff as he walked out into the storm.

Chapter Six

Jake hung up the phone; it didn't make him feel any better having talked to the sheriff. He was agitated not knowing Rich's exact whereabouts, and Jeff hadn't helped a bit. He realized that he had his hands full, but it seemed like a lousy excuse on his part.

Jake had lived on the Gannon Ranch since he was a kid. He had never married. Not that he hadn't thought about it; he just never got around to it. He often went into town and kept company with Sally the owner of the feed store. It was if they had their own understanding, at least on his end anyway. Sally was always hopeful and she cared a great deal for the old guy, but she just couldn't seem to get him to pop the question. Jake stood five foot nine in his stocking feet and almost five foot ten in his boots. He held his own with the ladies even with his looks weathered from years in the sun. Sally knew this and kept a watchful eye on all the other gals and most stood a bay from her, not wanting to tangle with her when she got that certain look on her face. Jake still had a healthy head of hair, and like his dad before him, it only had a skiff of gray around the ears.

He was the foreman of the Gannon Ranch. There was no doubt about that in his mind. He'd been such since he had worked for Rich's dad Bill Gannon many years ago. Besides, he reckoned, he was the only permanent hired hand, so that kind of left him in full command. When Rich's dad had died of cancer a few years back, he had asked him to take good care of his boy and watch out over him. So that made him a surrogate dad in his mind and he acted as such, bossing Rich around and giving commands like any dad would do.

Most often Rich would listen and not argue, except when he got tangled up with Mary and that was a battle Jake just didn't win. Mary was beautiful, he'd give her that alright, but that was all. He remembered trying to approach the subject with Rich and he was told not only to mind his own damn business but to drop it. The look on Rich's face made him back off. Mary was poison, the old man was sure of that. But he didn't dare to carry on with this thought openly for fear of losing the friendship he held dear to his heart. Nope, he wasn't about to say anything.

The old saying, beauty is as beauty does, fit her quite nicely, and it irritated the old guy to no end. He and Sally had often argued over Mary. Sally telling him that it was none of his business, and to stay out of it. Sally always won the argument, as he knew she was right. So he kept a civil tongue in his mouth, but mumbled under his breath a lot.

When Rich's Dad had passed away, they had almost lost the ranch, what with all the medical bills and such. But because of the imprint training Jake had begun with each new foal they had, and the hours spent on each, the ranch had pulled itself out of the red and was making real good money. Keeping a tight budget had put money in the bank, and each summer they were able to hire a couple of hands to help work the place. Rich liked working with the cows, so he left the horse dealings to Jake. Every horse they had or that was sold was as gentle as a pup, and Jake felt a sense of pride as each one left.

The ranch itself was about two-hundred acres and set just a hill from Bess Cramer, a little spit of a woman. Jake liked her a lot better, yup, a whole lot better than Mary and had said so once, only to get a dirty look by Rich and told to keep his mind on the ranch. Jake suspected he'd hit a subject that was close, too close to Rich's thoughts.

Rich knew that he was right and this bothered him, so he would get in his face and barked back at him. But for now he knew the subject was closed. *There were plenty of reasons, yes siree,* thought Jake, *not to like Mary.* She was no good and he knew it. That was a fact in his mind, but one of them Jake knew he could never speak about, not to Rich, or anyone else for that matter.

Late one afternoon when Jake was finishing up his work with Abby, a new foal, Mary came out in the skimpiest see-thru top she could find. He ignored her for the most part. Then she got right in his face and began rubbing herself on him. It made him sick to his stomach and he saw red. He grabbed her hard on her arm and pushed her away, then he got in her face. "You ever try that again, slut, and I'll see you in hell first, lady," and he threw her to the ground and walked away.

Then, when Mary came up missing that day, he felt scared, scared like he'd never felt before. He couldn't say he'd been with Rich or Rich with him, as he was just getting back from down below. The piece of land owned by the Gannon ranch in Cottonwood, California was in need of fence repair and he had elected to go.

He had pulled in with his truck and horse trailer and he swallowed hard. There were cop cars all over the place. Crime scene tape fenced around the house, noise from the sheriffs' radio was blaring and a sight he thought he never would see—Rich being shoved into a cop car and his hands being shackled in hand cuffs. He felt a sickness deep in the pit of his stomach, and for a brief moment Jake wondered if the arguing had finally gotten out of hand and Rich had actually killed her. Then he dismissed the thought, knowing the kid just didn't have it in him. He never will forget that, drops of blood everywhere, tempers flared and the sight of Rich being hauled off. It stuck in his mind like a piece of raw hamburger going up and down his throat.

Now Jake was worried for a whole new reason. Rich should have been back long before now. He'd grown up in this country so he knew that big storms could catch you off your guard. Jake looked out the window again and said a silent prayer to the ole white haired fellow on his horse in the sky. "Just make sure he's all right," he said.

This storm was scaring him; it was like nothing he had seen in a long while. The wind was up to fifty-five mile an hour and it was a cutting bitter cold. It brought with it flurries of snow that were piling up so fast that the drifts had began to stack up everywhere. By now Rich usually had phoned him, but the phone was silent. Jake had called Bess thinking he might have gone back there, as Rich had mentioned that he was going to see if she needed anything from town. Bess was kegged up pretty good from the conversation he had with her. He was careful not to alarm her or to show he was really worried, though he was sure he had heard a worried note in her voice when she spoke. He suspected he was right in thinking she was sweet on Rich. She was the only one he could ever really remember being allowed to call Rich by his formal name Richard and get away with it. He would just get a slight grin on his face and not say a word. *Well,* he thought to himself, *where are you Rich?*

Chapter Seven

Bess sat at her table thinking. She loved this country, even when the snow was so deep, so cold, and so miserable that it made your bones ache. But it wasn't like this all the time, and it sure did get into your soul. The summertime held the smells that lingered in your mind when the winter winds would blow. Sounds of the crickets and frogs in the air when the first spring rains fell. Walking among the pines, the desert sagebrush, or the laughter of children playing in a schoolyard because they enjoyed the freedom of uninterrupted play. Things were definitely fresher, cleaner, and more gentle than from the places Bess had been before she came back to her father's world. Things she had forgotten had existed. The things she had really missed. It had been a tough decision to make when she decided to come back here to live. Not so much the leaving the big city, but the memories of her dad, his saying you will never make it. When in truth he never really wanted her to go and really she never really did fit in in the big city. Bess knew people could be failures in all walks of life. It just depended on how you perceived yourself, and she did not define herself as a failure. She felt all along she belonged to this country, but she had just wanted to spread her wings a little, see new things, and expand her mind. She was never given the opportunity to help her dad to see these things in this light; he was gone before the blink of a eye.

The wind brought her back to the moment and she stoked up the fire once more. The two lanterns needed filling, she reminded herself. She lit the lantern she had hung in the kitchen window earlier and turned it up. The lights were still flickering on and off, and she was sure at any moment it would be in the off decision, and she did not want to be unprepared. Her dog Rocky had been whining and fussing for about an hour.

Maybe, just maybe, my mare is about to foal, she thought to herself. *I need to get out and check things in the barn anyway*. Wrinkling up her nose, she bundled up with every piece of warm clothing she could find. Bess knew enough not to be caught out in this without being bundled up good.

She called the dog. "Come on, Rocky, you're going to be my guide," she said. She knew that he would take her straight to the barn. He had made the trip many times and in some of the worst weather she had seen, and this was no exception. She put on his collar and leash, and opened the front door. It flew open once more with a slam; the wind catching it, and the snow furiously blowing in onto the floor. She grabbed the handle with both hands and pulled it shut. Gathering up the rope from the tack room, she tied one end around her waist and the other end to the porch. Bess clicked on her flashlight.

"Well, ole boy, here we go. Take me to the barn," she said as she stepped off the porch into the darkness. The wind whipped the snow, stinging her face with glass like shards. It hurt worse than she could remember it being in the past. She wondered if somehow she had lost her mind as she stepped out in the freezing cold night. *Surely this will let up,* she thought as she trudged along in the drifts of snow. Bess felt her way carefully and walked at a slow pace, counting on her dog to find the way. After what seemed like hours, she came to the fence that was connected to the barn. Pulling on the leash, the dog stopped.

"Hold on, boy," she shouted above the howl of the storm. "Let me tie up the rope." Wrapping it around several times she finally tied it up with a square knot making sure it was secure. "It's so cold out here," she muttered to herself as she picked up the leash. The fence had icicles all across the top of the boards, and each time she touched them her gloves soaked up the cold and wet. Her flashlight was getting dimmer as she made her way toward the barn. Then, as if this night couldn't get worse, the light on the outside of the barn went out.

"Well, there goes the electricity, Rocky," she said under her breath. "At least we still have our flashlight." It was completely dark in the direction of the barn. Bess didn't scare easily, but suddenly she never felt so alone. The thought came to her suddenly that she could die out here and not a soul would know. And no one would particularly care. Her body began to shake, frightened for the situation she had put herself in. The cold was setting in fast and she had come too far to turn herself around. *Besides,* she reasoned, *it wasn't that much farther. Then again why does the barn seem like a million miles away. Dad, I wish you were here,* she thought. Then her flashlight quit.

"CRAP," she said, " NOT NOW, NOT NOW!" She banged it hard against her hand. It came on, then it went off, came on, then off again, only this time it wouldn't come back on.

"Dang it, what am I going do?"

Rocky sensed she was frightened. He tugged and pulled her in a direction that seemed to her to be all wrong. Tears started coming down her face; she wasn't feeling very brave just now. The tears left a biting cold on her face as soon as the wind and snow hit them. *Stop pitying yourself,* she thought. *You could get us both killed.* She wiped away her tears, deciding to trust this ole dog who always seemed to know his way.

Suddenly Rocky stopped. She wondered why, and because she couldn't see, she felt her way. They had reached the barn. She felt a sense of relief. Bess stumbled, but caught herself and found the door. She kicked the snow out from in front of it as she pulled on the door handle.

"Thank you, God," she said as it gave way and opened part way. She squeezed through the door, and the dog followed. He was whining and moaning louder now. It sounded more like a howl.

"You poor ole dog, I'm so sorry I got you into this," she said, "We'll light the lantern and check on the mare and then we'll get the hell out of here. Okay?"

Bess felt her way to the lantern, reaching just below it. Her fingers touched the box of matches and something moved. She screamed, then laughed, realizing it was probably a mouse. Then her laughter became almost hysterical. She began to cry again. It seemed uncontrollable, the sobbing, her body shook and she thought again about her dad and wished he were there to comfort her. Then her thoughts shifted to Richard and how strong he seemed, how much he reminded her of her dad.

Come on, girl, this just isn't going to get it. She reached into the box of matches and pulled out one and struck it on its side. "Ahhhhhhhh, let there be light," she said.

Chapter Eight

Rich had left Bess's place with his pickup truck just a coughing and wheezing and he was feeling like a sixteen-year-old. Every time he was around her it was like this big rush. It felt like the beginning of a courtship with the girl of his dreams. He knew he didn't have a right to feel these things, and yet, it was like his first love. This draw he felt toward her was something that had consumed him from the first time his eyes lit on her, causing him to look for her consciously and unconsciously wherever he was. He found this to be true in the grocery store, drugstore, or even when he was at the feed store. He would step up in the line where she was, and pretend it was the only place left he could possibly go. She made him feel young, handsome, and special, and that was without even trying.

When her eyes would light on him, he would feel warm inside and a touch of being worthwhile. He couldn't seem to get enough of her. It was like being intoxicated when he was with her. He had thoughts about her day and night, and how he would like to protect her, put his arms around that tiny waist and hold her. And, yes, even what it would be like to kiss her lips. He decided God had given her the most beautiful big blue eyes he had ever seen. He realized all this was impossible, that she did not belong to him and he was married.

"Ahhh yes…married," he said, shaking his head, "very married." Married to a woman who did not want him, who it seemed never did. *I was simply a challenge for her,* he thought. He felt sick inside every time he thought about it. "I tried," he said. "God knows I've tried so hard. Hell, she didn't even want her kids, our kids. How can people be made that way," he wondered. "Why is it that some are born empty inside, where do they come from?"

It wasn't genetic with Mary. Her folks were the salt of the earth, good, kind, and gentle people. The kind who would give you the shirt off their back when you were in need of help. The kind you could count on in a pinch, and Rich liked them. He didn't think Mary really ever liked herself. *How could she?* he thought. *When she was so full of poison.* He felt sad for her and for her family, and now she's been gone what, two whole months now, just up and disappeared vanished with no trace.

His thoughts drifted back to that day. He had been camped out with his horse for a couple of days working the far corner of the ranch. Rich liked working alone. He had sent Jake to Cottonwood, California, about two weeks before to a piece of property he owned there. John, the hand he had hired, phoned and had said he could use some help with the repairs of the fence. They had just shipped all their cattle to that property to winter out, and so Jake said he would go. The morning before he headed up that hill, Mary and him had one hell of a fight. It had gotten so heated up he did something he thought he would never do. Without thinking he raised his hand and backhanded her. It brought blood to her nose and broke open her lip. She screamed at him to get the fuck out as her eyes moistened from the stinging pain.

"I'm sorry, Mary. I should never have raised a hand to you," he said as he reached to gently wipe away the blood on her face.

She backed away and screamed, "GO TO HELL!"

As he looked at her, he felt sick and disgusted that he could do such a thing to any woman. He felt ashamed. Looking at her, he lowered his head and quietly asked, "How come you never want to be around our kids, Mary? And how come you never ask about them? They are a part of you, of us?"

She turned to him and started laughing, shrill-like. "You poor, stupid, son of a bitch, you don't get it, do you?" she said. "They don't mean nothing to me, not a damn thing. They are just brats. HELL! I didn't even want them to begin with, but seeing how you needed to play dada," she said sarcastically, "I decided they could be pawns in my big plans. Shit, I didn't want to play mummy and daddy," she said as she sat on the bed holding a towel to her lip. "You are dumber than a post—a lot dumber than I thought."

He looked at her, his expression angry. "Why I ought to…"

"What," she said, "hit me again? You do and I'll slap you with an assault charge so fast it will make your head spin."

He started to walk away and turned around. "Did anyone ever tell you you're a bitch?"

"I've had worse said about me. Now if you don't mind, get the fuck out of here and leave me the hell alone."

"You have a disgusting dirty mouth," he said as he exited the bedroom. Thinking to himself, he shook his head. *Why do I even waste my breath.*

He headed out to the barn and gathered up his gear, bedroll and nap sack, with food for a couple of days. He threw his saddle on ole JB, his favorite horse, and headed up the hill. Looking out over the valley, he drew in a deep breath and let his horse lead the way. He remembered feeling the tension in his shoulders and his head was pounding with the worst headache he'd had in a while. The time spent out working the fence line would do them both good.

He thought the separation would cool both their hot tempers. He was tired of fighting, bickering and of trying to make things work. He was tired of pretending that there was anything left between them but hate. Let's face it he was tired, just plum tired of playing the head games and dealing with all the worry attached to it. His body had begun to relax as he worked with the wire, stretching it to repair a hole made by the cows. He worked up a sweat and it felt good to him, and as long as he was doing this, his mind did not have time to think about all that faced him when he returned home to the ranch.

When the nighttime fell and the stars were out, he found his mind would wander over the hill to Bess. *She is so opposite from Mary*, he thought. *She's a different kind of beautiful; the kind that glowed when she smiled. She liked to cook.* He knew that and she was good, he had tasted a couple of the dishes that she had brought to the grange meetings.

And when one of the Granger girls got married there last year he remembered the dance he had with her. The old time fiddlers were playing and Shorty sang an old-fashioned love song. He pulled her close, holding her hand in his, close to his heart. His breathing had become heavy, like a weight had been put there. He could smell her hair and he lost himself in her at that moment. It had felt like he could stay in her arms all night, that is until Mary saw them and came up and made a big scene about needing him right away. That is, if Miss Bess could excuse them, she had said sarcastically. He was mad and embarrassed, and had apologized, saying another time perhaps. Bess had smiled sweetly and said sure no problem she was needed in the kitchen anyway. She had left them standing in the middle of the dance floor in what looked to everyone like a heated argument, and headed for Sally next to the kitchen door.

He remembered being furious when he found out it was just an excuse of Mary's to get him away from Bess. He decided that it was better for Bess that he not ask for another dance. It would only have caused trouble for her. The men had brought their own bottles and the women had a few of their own stashed here and there. The laughter had rung out, bouncing off the walls that night. The music was sweet with old-fashioned waltzes, lots of good food and drink to last the night away. That party had lasted until the wee hours, with the music the fiddlers played and a shivery for the newly wed couple to end the evening.

He thought about all these things when he sat by his evening fire. It gave him time to reflect on all he had done and what he needed to do, and best of all were his thoughts of Bess. This was the time no one could steal from him, his thoughts were his own. But all too soon his work was done and he was on his way back to the ranch.

He loved being out here in this beautiful place. Juniper had a wonderful smell all its own even before you burned it. It made your lungs feel clean, like you wanted to take a deep breath and hold it. He loved the tall pines and sagebrush, the night sounds, and the fact that you could count on the moon. This made him smile. It gave way to the hope that things could be different, but all right somehow. For a moment he thought about the possibilities. Maybe, just maybe.

The closer he came to reaching the ridge the more he thought about Mary and everything they had said. He thought about it long and hard and knew that it wouldn't work. He thought he had loved her once, and he had hoped to make it work, but it just couldn't work for them. She didn't want it to. Besides, he knew he had feelings for Bess, though he would never act on them. Mary loved no one but herself and it was over for the both of them, he knew this. As much time as he had put in his marriage, it couldn't continue on with this horrible hate they had for each other. He decided that it was time to talk divorce. It was the only option left to them, short of killing her.

He returned to the barn at about three thirty in the afternoon. When he brushed J.B. down he gave him some oats and water, and hung the rest of his gear up in the tack room. He checked to see if the Miller's boy Jason had come over as promised and taken care of the other horses in their stalls. They all looked good, and he had brushed them down too.

"Hmmmmm," he said, "perhaps it's time to think about giving that young man a raise. He's done a really good job," he said, nodding his head. "He's dependable, very dependable…"

In his gut he hated this, he said to himself as he headed up to the house. But he knew if he didn't put a stop to this ugly marriage, he would be responsible for scars, emotional scars, on their kids.

When he walked out of the barn, he saw that Mary's car was in the driveway. This surprised him, as she was seldom home at this hour. As he approached the front gate, he felt a little uneasy; it was swinging open in the breeze. He glanced down and saw a few dried blood spots on the cement walk, and then he realized the front door was wide open. His stomach felt queasy. Stepping inside, he called to Mary. No answer. All he heard was dead silence, and the sound of the gate banging outside in the wind. He noticed more blood on the floor. Walking through the living room he took note that everything was a mess. Books on the floor, a lamp turned over, drawers pulled out, a chair dumped.

"MARY!" he shouted. He started to panic. "Mary, answer me," he hollered as he ran to the kitchen. Blood was in the sink, on the floor and the counter. He ran upstairs looking in all the rooms. Their room had been tossed, the bed was a mess, clothes torn out of the closet and on the floor, a jewelry box dumped over and spread in every direction. He ran downstairs, his throat was dry and he was shaking. He thought maybe she was hurt real bad and lying outside on the ground. He ran to the front door screaming her name, running so fast he lost his balance and ran smack into deputy Sam causing them to fall ass over tea kettle onto the ground.

"Hey, what's your hurry? What are you running from?" said Sam suspiciously as he picked himself up and dusted off his clothes. Sam did not like Rich. In fact, he thought he was stepping in on his territory, namely Bess.

Rich's shirt was soaked with sweat. He was flustered and out of breath…he tried to explain things to Sam hurriedly. And as he talked, he stepped off the porch toward the corner of the house, and Sam reached out and grabbed him by the shirt and shoved him down in the porch swing. Rich started to get up and Sam blew.

He said, "You're not going nowhere, boy. You just sit right there until the sheriff gets here, or do I have to put my the cuffs on you?"

"No, you stupid dickhead, but don't you think she might be laying out there somewhere while you sit here and wait for the sheriff?"

Sam moved without thinking. He struck Rich in the stomach with such force it knocked the wind out of him and took his breath away. Then he backhanded him, hitting him in the mouth, causing his lip to bleed.

His stomach was in knots, his anger beyond belief. But Rich thought to himself as he caught his breath, *If I react he'll get me for assault and it would be his word against mine.* Then he thought, *What the hell,* and with one powerful blow he knocked deputy Sam out cold.

The sheriff arrived just in time to see his deputy, Sam, knocked out cold…he had also been privy to what Sam had just done. He just shook his head. He knew Sam had a temper and he also knew that he hated Rich Gannon. He had said as much many times. The sheriff radioed headquarters letting them know he had arrived.

An anonymous tip had come in that the front door to the Gannon ranch was wide open and no one was around…the tipster also said there was blood on the walkway. Jeff picked up his mike again. "Yeah, this is Sheriff Baldwin, could you give me the ETA on Detective Smith and Crane?"

"ETA in ten, Sheriff," the radio blasted.

"Thanks, and ten four, Eva," said the sheriff.

Rich could hear all this as he sat waiting for the sheriff to get out of his car. The sheriff walked through the gate and up to the front porch, carefully stepping around the blood splatters on the walk.

"Okay, Rich, want to tell me what's going on?" he said as he reached down and felt the side of the deputy's neck.

Rich began by telling him his story, beginning with his argument with Mary and ending with, "And so I coldcocked him. I didn't appreciate him hitting me. And I damn well would like to know what happened to her. Fight or no fight, she's missing and I have two little kids to answer for."

"Well, the detectives will be here in a minute," he said as he handcuffed Rich to the porch swing, "Why don't you just sit here while I have a look around?" said the sheriff.

Stepping off the porch, the sheriff went into the house. Rich sat there, he realized of the gravity of his situation. It hit him like a ton of bricks and he knew this didn't look good. Maybe he shouldn't have told Jeff about the fight he had with Mary. He thought, *MAYBE I should have just kept my damn mouth shut, and my hands to myself.*

By the time Sheriff Baldwin had made a pass through the house and arrived back at the front door, Deputy Sam was starting to wake up.

"What the hell?" he said, groggy-like, rubbing his chin. "What the hell happened here?"

"Never mind, Sam," said the sheriff. "You'll be all right and we'll talk about this later. In the meantime I want you to put tape up to protect this area until we figure this thing out. Rich, I'm going to walk you through the house carefully," he said as he undid the cuffs from the swing. "I want you to tell me if anything could be missing."

Sam was pissed, it was obvious as he stormed off muttering to himself. He began wrapping tape around the front and back of the place as the sheriff and Rich did a walk-thru, careful not to touch anything.

Rich took a careful inventory of everything as he and Jeff examined each room. He told Jeff about the hidden money Mary had put away in the mattress and how he had found it while playing with his son. It was now gone, and though her jewelry box was spilled, he found only one item gone and that was a gold and diamond charm bracelet that Mary had once bought for herself. Two dresses and a coat, a pair of pants and a couple of shirts were missing. These he remembered as they were pieces he had bought for her himself.

They looked at the blood in the sink and talked about the fact she might have cut herself while trying to get ice out of the trays. Jeff was certain in his mind that there wasn't any foul play, but he was going to wait until the detectives arrived and see if they came to the same conclusion. Besides, he knew Mary and in his mind she could be a bottle full of trouble.

Jake pulled up with his truck and trailer as the sheriff was putting Rich into his car. "What the hell is going on here?" he asked.

The sheriff and Sam where screaming at one another.

"Sam!" Jeff screamed, "I said we will finish this discussion back at the office."

"Like hell we will," screamed Sam back. "Just what makes you think nothing happened here? You know he assaulted an officer…me."

"Yeah, I know," said Jeff, his face angry, "and would you JUST like to explain to everyone the assault you put on him first, Sam? I saw it all, everything and I mean everything that happened. I saw it. Now shut up and get in your car and get the hell out of here before I put you in cuffs."

Jake asked again, "What the hell is going on here?"

Jeff looked up at Jake. "We have to take him in until we get this sorted out. Mary's missing, Jake, and the detectives are looking over the house. If you want to follow us in that will be fine."

"Yeah, I'd like that," said Jake. "I'll unhitch this trailer and be right along." "You okay, Rich?" asked Jake.

"Yeah, I'm fine, just fine," he said. Closing his eyes, his mouth was still bloody from the fight earlier and it was starting to bruise.

This worried the sheriff. "Okay, buddy, see you in just a bit?" he said, giving Sam a dirty look as he walked past by his car.

Sam looked up and said, "What the hell you looking at?"

Sheriff Baldwin was as quick as lighting as he ran up to Sam's door and slammed his leg in it.

Sam moaned, then he growled loudly, "HEY!"

"Hey, yourself," said the sheriff. "Now get the hell out of here, I won't tell you again!"

Sam didn't say any more, he just closed the door, turned the key, looked straight ahead and drove off screeching his tires on the gravel in the road as he left, letting them all know just how pissed he was.

Chapter Nine

When it was finally decided that Mary's disappearance was just that, and that she had just walked off on her own, leaving behind most of her things, not telling or informing anyone, not even her parents of her whereabouts, it was a big relief to Rich. He didn't like being accused of her murder. He did not have a valid alibi, at least not one he could prove anyway. And the fact he had admitted to the sheriff that he and Mary had fought that morning did not help his situation one bit. Mary had left, leaving him holding the bag, and he wasn't so sure she hadn't found it all funny and was laughing about it somewhere. He was positive, though, she would show up when she ran out of money.

Mary thought he didn't know about the money she was stashing under her mattress. And in any other normal situation he might not have known where it was, except one morning when Mary was gone, he and Tylor were wrestling in their bedroom and the mattress was shoved aside as they played. He was astounded when he found the money she had put there. He put it back so she wouldn't know he had found it, and at that moment Rich had decided not to confront her with it. He had other plans. He knew she was taking it out of their bank account, as he kept careful books on the ranch account. But until then he wasn't sure where she had put it. It was one more thing that put a wedge between them.

He had been feeling dead inside when it came to Mary for a long time now. It didn't seem to matter what he said or what he did, it wasn't right. To know Mary had done this for her getaway money had made him feel sick inside, and to hide it from him when he would have given it to her anyway. Well, it hurt unbearably. He had wanted this to work and he knew his spurts of anger were not adding to any healing, it only seemed to make it worse. *We are destroying each other*, he thought. *God help us!*

His thoughts ran rampant as he headed toward town. The wind was shaking his old pickup truck making it rattle and creak. The snow swirls were coming down in big flakes now. His radio was playing one of Faith Hill's songs "If I Should Fall Behind." *Nice,* he thought. *Great voice.*

He slowed down as he approached town, turning on Roberta Avenue. His friend Jerry had a couple of tires he had traded for quarter ton of hay. He had looked at the tires a couple weeks earlier and they were in real good shape. *It was a good swap*, he told himself as he pulled into his driveway.

Jerry came out all bundled up, pulling his coat up around his neck. The storm was getting messy and the wind was making the snowdrift in places.

"Jerry, where do you want this hay?" asked Rich.

Jerry motioned with his hand and hollered, "Back it up against this shed."

Rolling back up his window, Rich backed up to his shed. He jumped out and started to unload the hay. Jerry got in the back and helped him and in no time it was done. Jerry opened up the door to the shed and rolled out the tires. Rich grabbed one tire and Jerry the other, lifting them into the truck.

"These are in real good shape," he said to Jerry, reaffirming what he already knew.

Jerry just grinned. "I told you I'd make you a fair deal," he said.

"That you did," he said, "that you did."

The wind and snow had closed the tracks in behind him. Looking up he saw this as he slammed the tailgate shut. "Well, Jerry, I've got to get on the road," he said. "This weather is not fit for man or dog. Thanks again."

Jerry's face looked concerned, "Be careful, it sure don't look to let up anytime soon."

Rich got in his truck and turned the key over. It dragged, giving a rrr...rr. "Come on, ole girl, don't give up on me now." Then a vrooooooommm, and it started. He waved his hand at Jerry as he pulled out of the driveway.

The roads had about three inches on them now, and it was getting deeper by the minute. The hour was getting late. Rich had not expected it to take so long getting to town and delivering Jerry's hay. It had been a last minute decision to bring it in and deliver it in the first place. Now it caused him to be out in this storm longer than he anticipated.

Swinging his truck into Sally's Western Feed Store, he was careful how he parked, backing up to the loading ramp to within a foot or so making it easier to load the feed he was after. He jumped out of the truck and walked up the steps, wading through the heavy snow. Sally waved at him as he passed the window and he smiled. The wind howled and gusts blew the door open.

"How's it going, cowboy?" she asked. "What brings you out in this nasty stuff?"

"Well, it wasn't my intention to be caught in this," he said, stroking his chin, "You know, it wasn't snowing when I left the ranch. It just threatened to that's all." Laughing, he dusted off the snow on his clothes.

"What can I do for you today, Rich?" she said.

"I need three sacks of chicken feed, two for Bess Cramer, and one for me. I told her I'd pick it up for her while I'm in here."

Sally just grinned to herself. She knew that even if he wasn't aware of it, he was definitely sweet on Bess. "Sure," she said, "anything else?"

"Yes, do you have those real warm gloves in stock. The ones you got from Stockman's last year. They were real warm."

"I'm just about sold out, but I have…let's see…" she said as she reached into one of the shelves, "…two pair mediums and one pair large. What size are you?"

"I'm probably closer to a medium, Sally. I don't like my gloves to be to loose on my hands. What about warm vests?"

"Come here," she said. Grabbing his arm, she took him to the rack of winter clothing that sat near the back. "Here, try this one on."

It was a black western down vest with snaps and pockets on both front sides. He slipped it on. It fit perfectly.

"Looks good on you," she said.

"Sold," he said. "Thanks, I'll wear it out. Now about that feed."

He loaded up after paying Sally for his goods and headed down the road. He didn't like the looks of this weather. It was getting worse by the minute and darkness, well, let's just say he was losing the light, and he had one more item to get.

Chapter Ten

The flakes were so large they were mesmerizing and making him feel drowsy. He felt hypnotized. It reflected the lights back in his eyes, blinding him, causing him to change them from dim to bright, bright to dim, and back to dim again. It was slow going for his old pick up, managing a creeping five miles an hour. The wind shook and rattled the metal on his old truck, and it came in spurts, reminding him that he wasn't in charge.

Maybe I should have stayed in town, he thought. *I could have stayed at the feed store. Sally probably would have put me up for the night in her room out back.* "I remember Jake talking about it," he said aloud as his voice echoed in the truck. *Humm*, he thought, *that one time when Jake got loaded. Sally wouldn't put him up at her place. Said she wouldn't send him home in that condition either, so she dumped him on the cot, covered him up, took his keys, and said, "See you in the morning." Jake just laughed and said, "I deserved it, and I guess you know I was apologizing for it in the morning."* Rich grinned to himself, shaking his head. I don't know why he doesn't just make an honest woman of her. Anyone can tell Sally's crazy about him.

Just then a gust of wind rattled the truck, bringing him back to the cold reality of where he was. He hadn't seen any lights for a while, but he realized with this white out it would be hard to see anything unless you were right on top of it. He felt disoriented and wasn't sure if he were still heading in the direction of home or if he had by passed the road somehow.

I wish I could crawl in somewhere hide and sleep. I'm so tired, sleepy…he thought. His shoulders ached, the stress of fighting with the blinding snow was more than his body could manage. He rubbed his neck with his hand, trying to work it loose from the tension he felt. *Oh man, I wish that spring would hurry up and get here*, he thought. *I think I've had enough of this to last me a lifetime.* His eyes were getting weary from fighting the white flakes of snow blowing in his face against the windshield. His wipers screeched and moaned trying to keep up with the pace as it came down. He could feel the drifts of snow as they jerked the truck back and forth in the road.

Rich caught his eyes closing and he jerked them open. *I've got to keep awake...keep awake,* he thought. The humming and rattle of his truck was like a lullaby, softly singing to him. He thought, *Maybe if I hum to myself.* He started to hum, he could feel himself drifting, his eyes closing.

"NO! that won't work," he said as he stopped humming. Reaching for the handle he rolled the window down. The snow blasted in so bad he couldn't see, and it was cold, so he rolled it back up. *Damn, I wish this night was over,* he thought. Then he felt it again, the uncontrollable urge to close his eyes. *Sleepy...so sleepy...think about today,* he thought. *Keep your mind busy. Ahhhh less see, Sally got me the gloves,* he whispered as his eyes shut, *and, and, and it's so quiet,* as he exhaled and drifted. *So...quiettttt sweet, sweet quiet.* He spoke softly, "Just a little...close eyes for jus a...sec...can't...keep..." Heavy, feels good, he thought.

SUDDENLY, he felt the jolt of his seat belt as it tightened across his chest. The ground was flooding through the window, and his body was rolling over and over and over. Windows shattered, the sound of metal grinding like fingernails on a chalkboard, snow blasted past his face and he felt a sharp pain in his chest, then he hit his head. Then silence. Dead silence.

Chapter Eleven

The SVE electric company and the BCB phone crew had been out in the storm working all night trying to restore most of the downed electric and phone lines due to the severe weather and one eighteen wheeler that had biffed it sliding into the power poles. They had been working in the cold and wet mess and it proved to be very slow going. When most of the repairs had been taken care of, the crew gathered at Ed and Irene's Double A Café. Some of the crew went home and others stayed for more than coffee, for the food was always real good, and the conversations always great.

"George, would you like some more coffee?" asked Kathy

"No, I believe I've had about all I can hold. Thanks anyway, my dear," he said, smiling. "Say, did you hear anything about Rich Gannon being missing?"

"No," she said, "is he?"

"Well, I don't know, but I heard tell Jake's been looking for him. If he's missing out in this storm, it's not good."

"Yeah, I know," she said. "It's real bad out there."

"Say, George, not to change the subject or anything, but you want to come to my place tonight? It's closer than your place and you won't have to drive all the way out to the west side in this storm."

"I'd like to. But I'm not sure about it, Kathy. You know how people are here, and how they talk. I don't want to mar your reputation."

"It's perfectly legit. I'll have you know, Mr. George, I wouldn't dream of tarnishing your reputation. Besides, I have a spare room in the house. And I promise I won't touch you."

"It's not me worrying about YOU touching me, hon. It's me worrying about ME touching you," he said.

"OHHH," she said quietly. "So, will yah? Come anyway that is?"

"Tell you what, Kathy. What time do you get out of here?"

"In about an hour. Why?"

"Well, I'll come, but only if I can escort you home. You know I'm on call with these phones out, so I may not be there long."

"Okay, you sure you don't want anything, George?"

"I'm full," he said patting his belly, "but I guess I'll take another bowl of that hot chicken soup and one more refill of coffee," he said, stretching and yawning. "By the time I get through with them you aught to be ready to go. Okay?"

"Okay," said Kathy. She smiled as she dipped him a steaming bowl of hot soup out of the pot and picking up the coffee, she poured him another cup.

The storm was relentless. It raged on, wet, cold and angry covering the vehicles that were pulled up out front. When it came time for George and Kathy to leave, they had to get help to back out. Several of the guys came out to push and George was grateful. Kathy was embarrassed, however, as she hadn't expected to have this much fanfare when she left. George reminded her they would only think she was getting a ride home in this terrible storm. *I've seen some mighty bad storms, but this one's real bad,* he thought as he pulled out into the street, driving the lady home.

Chapter Twelve

When Rich woke up, he felt the cold against his face, his clothes were wet, and he was in a lot of pain. His mind wouldn't let him focus on the how or why he was there. He was disoriented and his mind was fuzzy. He laid there for a moment with his eyes closed and in pain.

"How long have I been here?" he grunted, then he thought, *Where am I?* He tried to connect the dots in his mind. He started to feel around. "Ohhhhhh," he moaned with pain, "my chest hurts." Then he touched his eye. "Ahh," he groaned, as he sucked in his breath and jerked his hand away.

The wind howled and snow was filling in fast around him. He felt around to see if he could find his flashlight. *It should be under the seat*, he thought, *but nothing feels right.* Rich reached for his seat belt and released the latch. He was in luck he thought as it gave away. His body fell and he doubled up in pain, crying out.

"Damn it," he said as he gasped. He hadn't realized he was upside down. *How in the hell did I get myself into this mess?* Then he remembered coming from town and he thought, *Did I fall asleep at the wheel...could I have hit a berm in the road? You idiot,* he thought. *Who cares? I need to get the hell out of here before I die.*

Again he searched for the flashlight, but very gingerly, for his body was in a weakened state. His fingers felt carefully as he didn't want to cut them from the broken glass scattered across from where he lay. He decided it was fruitless to continue his search for his light and gloves.

It is dangerous to stay here, he thought. Crawling out the window, he could see a slight halo of a light coming from one of the headlights buried deep in the snow.

Looking around, Rich took in his situation. He knew he needed to get out of this storm and fast. The few moments he had stood outside his truck getting his bearings the snow had packed thickly on his clothes. His ankle felt tender, one hand had a sprain from what he could tell, and it hurt to breath. *Boy, what kind of a mess did you get yourself into this time?* he thought.

Then Rich saw a light. It seemed to be only a couple of miles away if he cut across the field. *That has to be someone's ranch shed, something maybe I can get in out of the cold for the night,* he thought, and so he took his first step, then his next and the one after that.

Rich kept a steady pace. He counted the steps, one, two, three. It seemed like hours and it kept going on and on and on toward the light. His body felt like it was getting warmer and his mind seemed to be a blur. His body was playing tricks on him. Shivering, he thought, *Didn't I just talk to Jake? He said I'll be fine.* Then he thought he had made it to the light, but the light went out. Then there was an angel. *She looked a lot like Bess, you know. She was crying, but angels don't cry, do they?* Then he was in the snow again, and it was howling. *Does the wind howl? Or was that a dog? I just want to sleep,* he thought. *What's that scraping sound I hear? Someone's crying again. Snow. Cold by my ears. Someone's pulling me? Who's laughing? Why? Clothes off! Don't have mind. Sleepy. ...angel kisses...angel's body warm. Am I still walking through the snow? I'm cold, so cold. My feet are stinging. I hurt. Angels give sweet water. Angel's body warm. She looks like someone I know.* He tried to see. *Do I know you, angel? She's not wearing clothes. Can I hold you, angel? You feel warm.* He reached out and put his arms around his angel. He touched her hair and fell into a deep but painful sleep.

Chapter Thirteen

Jake had fed all the animals, latched and buttoned up all the doors in the barn. He knew this was some storm coming, the likes of which he had not seen in some time. When he finished, he headed up to the main house, fighting the wind, snow, and cold. He stamped his feet when he got to the back door going on in to the porch. When he got inside the kitchen, Jake poured himself a cup of coffee, sat down at the table and listened to the wind howl. The snow was still coming down fast and furious. It had drifted some over the fence line in places. Jake sat there reflecting about what Bess had said about rounding up extra lights, water, and such. "Not a bad idea," he said aloud as he sipped his coffee. *Anyway, the lights had been flickering all afternoon,* he thought, so Jake set about the task of filling everything he could find with water.

He dug up a bucket or two, a few pots and pans and some jugs he'd found in the pantry. Then he began to look for candles and lamps, and while in the process, he found a couple of lanterns. They were filled, so all he had to do was light them, and that was just what he decided to do.

The fire in the living room was down to a flicker, so Jake grabbed an couple of sticks of lodgepole and threw them in the stove. They crackled and popped as the fire rose to a warm glow again. Jake felt as if a hundred years had passed since the morning had began. He was tired and drained, and he had decided that there was nothing more he could do to find Rich.

Anyway, it would be stupid, just plain stupid, to go out in this and search for him. Rich was going to have to rely on his own to get him through. Besides, Jake reasoned, *he had said a prayer, such as it was, to the old white haired man in the sky. He might listen to him just this once, not that he hadn't in the past, but he wasn't big on prayer. He only did when he thought it should count big, cause he didn't want to bother the big guy with the small stuff. He hoped that it was enough get him through.*

He finally sat down in a chair facing the fire. The reflection flickering on the wall made him realize that at some point the lights had gone out, and he wasn't sure when. *Boy, I'm tired,* he thought as he sat in an overstuffed chair in front of the stove. He grabbed a quilt and threw it over his shoulders. Feeling warmed by the fire, Jake found himself drifting into a dream. "Please Lord," he said softly, "let him be all right," as he dozed into his dream.

His dream took him out into the cold and the snow. He could hear the wind howling. The snow was blinding, and ahead of him was Rich stumbling along at a slow pace. He was covered with the white stuff and icicles were hanging from his clothes. He looked as if he couldn't make another step. His body limp his eyes heavy and laden. *Oh, no,* thought Jake, squirming in his sleep, he moaned, turning in the chair and his blanket fell to the floor.

Jake reached out in his dream and touched Rich's shoulders he looked him straight in the eye and said to him "You can make it, you hear me? You'll be all right, Rich!" he shouted. He had shook his head as if he understood.

Then his dream spun, it whirled like in a hurricane and settled into Sally's place. He saw her cooking over her stove, *God, you know, she is so beautiful,* he thought.

"Would you like to get the plates, Jake?" she said. He took a whiff. *Mmmmm something sure smells good,* he thought. "Sure," he said as he placed them on the table. She set the lasagna down and lit the candles. Jake pulled out her chair and noticed that the lights from the candles flickered in her hair. Sally was talking, but he didn't hear a word she was saying. He could only watch as her lips moved as he was spacing off and his thoughts went to the realization he was in love with this wonderfully beautiful woman, and suddenly he didn't want to be alone anymore.

Reaching into his pocket, he pulled out a box. "Sally? Sally?" he mumbled aloud as he stirred in his chair. Jake opened his eyes slowly, trying to get his bearings. He suddenly thought as he shook his head, *I was only dreaming.*

He felt stiff as he stretched his arms and legs. He stood up and bent over to touch his boots, then he reached up, extending his arms and fingers, clasping them together and cracking his knuckles.

Jake decided to bring in more wood for the fire, so he headed for the back porch. He piled four or five sticks on his arms and quickly shut the door against the cold and wind. He stacked these by the stove fireplace, throwing in a couple. He decided to stay at the ranch house tonight. Anyway, there was nothing in the bunkhouse to freeze. Besides, if Rich did come home, this was the first place he would come. His thoughts drifted back to his dreams and he shook his head slightly, thinking how strange dreams can be sometimes.

Jake's stomach was growling and he thought about Bess's chicken. He sure could use some of that about now. Just thinking about it he could taste it and he was sure he could smell it. *Well, a can of soup would just have to do,* he thought, as he headed for the pantry.

He grabbed up the lamp that was sitting on the island in the kitchen and headed for the pantry. He opened the door, giving it a slight push. *It always stuck about midway,* he thought. It was stocked on both sides was about any kind of can food that you would need, everything from soup, canned meats, flour, sugar, mayonnaise, even soap and jam. He grabbed himself a can of soup and one can of meat. The light from the lamp flickered, giving the walls an eerie appeal.

Jake just shook off the chill he felt. Opening his can of soup, he set it on the flame and in no time he was sitting down to his evening meal. He reached over and picked up the phone. It was dead. "That was tooo much to hope for," he said aloud, as he hung it back up.

He set his dishes in the sink and wiped up his mess and headed for the living room. Jake grabbed another blanket from the closest by the door, and a pillow; he threw them on the couch. He was exhausted and he knew it. The hour was late and keeping awake was not an option. He had turned off the lamp in the kitchen and turned down the one in the living room.

The fire crackled, the house creaked, moaned and groaned. The wind was still fierce and it howled unmercifully. All these sounds were eerie on this night, but there was a rhythm to them as the snow slapped against the windowpanes. Jake could take no more as he covered up and laid his head on the pillow. His body responded to the warmth of the fire and the sounds of the night, and he drifted off into a deep sleep. This time his body and mind waiting for the sounds and colors that could only come from the morning light.

Chapter Fourteen

Bess stood still, frozen in time, as she realized that she was not alone in the barn. The lamp she had lit gave out light throughout and her horses whinnied acknowledging her presence. From the corner of her eye she caught sight of a frozen mound laying next to the bales of hay she had thrown down earlier. Gasping in surprise, she approached with caution. Rocky appeared to know who it was. He wagged his tail and whined, laying down next to the man. He looked as if he were dead. In fact, she was sure he was dead as she reached her hand down and turned him over. Just then she heard a low moan.

"Oh my God!" she said as she began to cry, then sob, putting her hand over her mouth. It was Richard. She put her arms around him and brushed some of the snow from his face. Her tears were blinding and droplets fell on her coat. Bess knew she had to get him out of the barn and into the house where it was warm—and fast. Laying his head down gently, she looked around and saw her saddle blankets and quickly jumped up and grabbed them to cover him up.

Then, realizing she could not physically pick him up and pull him like that, she spotted the sled she used to haul hay out to the cows every day. Pulling it up close to him, she rolled him up on it and covered him with the blankets. Tying him to it so he wouldn't fall off, she checked again to see that he was still breathing.

Bess set the lamp in the barn window and turned it up as far as it would go. Opening up the barn door, she had found an axe head and wedged it against the snow to hold the door open as she pulled him through. Fighting the wind and the snow, she was glad for the light in the window as she pulled and tugged at the sled.

Rocky and she backtracked all the way down the fence line until she got to the rope she had tied earlier. She decided the best way to do this was to tie the rope from the sled around her waist and pull hand over hand until she reached the house.

The snow was slapping her in her face, making it hard to see, but she felt very driven and wasn't about to give up. She knew that the end of the line was the house, and she just couldn't let him die.

Once again tears stung her face. *I'm in love with this man,* she thought, *and I don't have a right to be.*

Bess fell down in the snow. The wind was blowing so hard it was difficult for her to stand back up. Getting on one knee, she brushed the snow from her face. Bess could see the light in the window of the house. Feeling around, she found the rope once again and got to her feet. She felt the tug and the pull of the sled behind her, and after what seemed like hours they finally arrived at the house.

The wind howled and whistled behind them as Bess's door flew open. Grabbing the rope with both hands, she pulled him through the door, falling on her butt.

She laughed out loud, thinking, *If my dad saw this he would be rolling on the floor.* The more she thought on this, the more she laughed out loud. *Here, my door is wide open, snow coming down and blowing all over and I have a man in a sled flying across my floor.* Gathering her composure, she picked herself up and shut the door.

Now, she thought, *we have to get you warm.* Bess worked quickly. She unwrapped the horse blankets she had laid on him before she tied him down. His face was a solid white; his mustache was a frozen popsicle and his lips the color of blue.

He asked, "Are you my angel?"

She reached down, touched his face gently and kissed him once, then again and again. Tears fell from her eyes. "Maybe I am," she said and she kissed his lips. *They were so cold,* she thought. "You'll be all right," she said. "I'll take good care of you."

Bess jumped up and grabbed a stick of wood, threw it on the fire and closed the stove door. She knew from reading that he needed to get warm gradually and he needed sweet warm water because of the possibility of dehydration. The inside needed to get warm too. She poured water from the teakettle, cooling it to the right temperature and added sugar to it. She brought it to his lips.

"Drink," she said. "Come on, take a sip, that's right." As she tipped it up, he swallowed a little at a time.

The door to her bedroom was open. Bess pulled back the quilt and sheet on her bed. Richard was delirious. He mumbled, but she knew he was not going to be any help. She would have to do this all on her own.

She pulled the sled into her room and reaching under his arms, it took all her strength to lift him up into her bed. Once there, she stripped him of all his clothes. His feet were red and he complained to her that they were stinging.

Bess knew what she had to do, that there wasn't a choice. She quickly undressed and slid into the bed next to him. He was the coldest icicle she had ever touched in her life.

"Do I know you?" he said. She just smiled. "Are you my angel?"

Maybe I am, she thought.

He reached out and put his arm around her and he touched her hair and fell into a deep sleep.

Chapter Fifteen

Bess knew he had a high fever. His forehead was hot and wet with perspiration. She filled her water basin with cool water and dipped the wash cloth into it. She drizzled the water over his forehead and down his chest, cooling his body the best she knew how, doing this over and over through out the night. She worried that he might not make it.

Please don't let me get you out of this storm and lose you. "Lord, I've never dealt with anything like this before. Please guide me," she whispered. She tore up one of her old sheets and carefully wrapped it around this chest. He moaned every time she touched this area so she was sure he had either cracked his ribs, or they were bruised and sore. His wrist and one ankle were swollen, so she kept hot and cold packs to them all night until they looked like they had gone down.

He must have rolled his truck, she thought. *That's the only explanation there is for the bruises and cuts. I bet Jake is worried sick about him. Phones are out so I can't call him. Well, it will just have to wait.*

Richard would open his eyes every now and then. She was sure he didn't know where he was, as his eyes were glazed. *He'll need some dry clean clothes when he wakes,* she thought. *Dad's stuff is packed and still in the attic,* she thought. *They should be okay, 'cause I washed everything before I packed them away in bags and sealed them.*

Moments later she was opening his clothes box. Digging through them, she turned up the lantern so she could see the clothes better. He's about the same size as Dad, so that won't be a problem. They still look pretty good.

She set them on the chair by the bed and felt his forehead. He was tossing and turning fretfully in his sleep, flinging his arms and mumbling. Sometime she could make out what he was saying. It was about Mary and it wasn't nice.

Bess just sighed as she ran her fingers over his face and through his hair. She knew this was going to be a long night. Sometimes she would sit on the bed next to him cooling him off. Sometimes she would take a break and sit in her old rocker that sat in the room. She kept sponging his body until the wee hours of the morning and his fever finally broke. She was finally so exhausted that she pulled an afghan up around her shoulders and rocked, watching him sleep. She said a silent thank you to the man upstairs and gently, without knowing it, fell into a deep slumber.

Chapter Sixteen

Rich awoke with a jolt, his eyes trying to focus, his body in pain. It hurt to move. *I don't recognize this room,* he thought. *There's a pitcher in a bowl sitting on a dresser with a doily under it.* He wrinkled up his brow. "What the…" he said. On the wall he saw a hanging made of old barn wood a picture of a cowboy throwing his lasso over a calf. Then his eyes focused and he was looking at the closet, and hanging in it was a woman's dress and more.

He was puzzled, he had never been in this room. Then he carefully turned and his mouth went dry. Sitting on a rocker in her nightgown was Bess and she was sound asleep. She had a cover over her shoulders and she was breathing softly. He thought, *How did I get here?* He started to get out of bed and realized he didn't have any clothes on and he gathered the blanket around him.

His mind went back to his dreams and realized that he had not been dreaming. He laid there for a while and watched her breathe. *She's so little,* he thought, *beautiful, and giving, and she saved my life.* His heart swelled and he felt overwhelmed.

He decided it was getting cold in the house. He needed to build up the fire. He didn't want to embarrass her, and realizing the clothes next to the bed were for him, he painfully but quietly got out of the bed and slipped from the room, shutting the door so he could dress.

He felt weak, but it was so good to be alive. *Someone up there was watching over me,* he thought. After he built up the fire, he peeked out the window and saw the blizzard raging outside. He wondered how he had ever made it there and however in creation did that little spit of a woman get him out of the storm and into that bed. *Well, won't wonders ever cease?*

He slipped quietly back into her room and gently put his arms around her, lifting the tiny form up close to him. He could smell her hair. Careful not to wake her, he closed his eyes for a moment, and touched his face to hers, feeling the softness of her skin. She moaned and this startled him. Holding her close, he gently laid her down on the bed and without a second thought he tenderly kissed her on her forehead. He tucked her in carefully, and quietly slipped from the room.

Chapter Seventeen

Jake woke up with a start and took a look at his watch—7: 30. *Damn it, it's late*. He jumped up and pulled his socks on, buttoning up his shirt. He thought he heard a noise and a banging in the kitchen by the back door.

"Well, I'll be damned," he said out loud. Standing outside in the cold and wind knocking the snow off his boots was Mex.

"Come on in," he hollered. Jake grabbed the door and ushered him in. "What the heck are you doing out in this?" he asked

Mex dusted off his clothes before he stepped through the door. "Well, eets like dees senor. My peekup she stalled and lass night dee storm was bad. I could not walk home to my misses in dees, so I find your barn and build a fire een your bunkhouse. I crash lass night een your bed. I hope eet was okay. Yes?"

"Sure, Mex. I wouldn't want it any other way. I'm mighty glad for the company." He reached for the old Mexican's coat and helped him pull his overshoes off. "Let's get you by the fire, ole boy. Why don't you set yourself down a spell while I put on a pot of coffee?"

"Si, senor, dat would be mighty good."

Jake poured water from a gallon jug into the pot and emptied the last of the grounds out of the canister and set it on the stove, lighting it with a match. He opened another can of coffee and dumped it into the canister. Then he opened up the stove and added a piece of wood to the fire. By this time the coffee was perking. He poured two cups of coffee and handed one to ole Mex.

"Tank you, senor, dees ees such nice of you."

"You're welcome," said Jake.

"Senor, I confess and I hope you don't mind? But your animals they all are fed good, lots off water. Oh, and I geeve to your chickens also. They lay you numeral eggs, but I left dem by the door."

"Thanks," he said, "I appreciate that. I'm, well, I slept in too long this morning and it was later than I thought." Jake jumped up and headed for the back door. He retrieved the eggs and took a quick survey of the weather. It hadn't let up any and it didn't appear like it would any time soon. He turned around and almost fell over the old Mexican. He hadn't heard him coming.

The old guy just snickered. "You av to watch out for dees ole boy I can sneak up on you real quiet."

"That you can." Jake grinned.

The old guy looked in the bottom cupboard by the stove and pulled out a pan. He said, "You seet, senor, I cook, dat's the smallest I can do for you for saving my life."

Jake laughed, "I didn't save your life."

"Oh, but you deed, You see, when you left dee lantern to burn in dee barn I see dee light," he said as he crossed his body in the sign of the cross, "and dee Madonna she guide me to dees light. I would av died out dare if not for dee light. She watch out over me."

That brought a worried look to Jake's face and he looked away for a moment as if he were somewhere else.

Mex put a caring hand on Jake's shoulder and said, "He'll be okay, senor."

"Who?" said Jake

"Senor Rich, dees ees who you worry about, yes?" he said, shaking his head.

"How did you know?" he said

"Well," he said as he cracked the last egg into the pan, "eets very obvious that Senor Rich ees not heer, and you sat most of dees cold night up here alone. I look een your sink, dare's only dish for one. Yes?"

"Yes," said Jake

"Now," said Mex, "you get us two plates. I fix you up with good breakfast, si?"

"Si," said Jake, and he poured them both another cup of coffee. He grabbed the eating tools out of the drawer and set the table. It felt good to have company. Him and the ole Mex sat and ate, jabbering up a storm. They talked about imprint training. Mex asked a lot of questions and Jake filled him in with the answers.

Boy, that was good eats, he thought. *That old Mexican can cook.* "That's real good food, Mex. I haven't eaten that good in a while, thanks."

"No, tank you again, senor, for saving dees old Mexican from meeting his maker lass night. I was not prepared to gooooo, I av not confessed my seens and dat would av been barry barry bad. Perhaps dees ole boy is to get another chance. Yes?"

"Maybe you are, Mex!" he said. Jake looked at him and grinned. He couldn't stand it any longer, he had to ask. "Where and why did you get the name old Mex? Is that your real name?"

Shaking his head no, he said, "When I just come to dees great country," he said, waving his hands in the air, "I was a very young man. I had a hot chili temper and I got ento a lot of fights, trouble, big trouble. Well, one of dem almost took my life, senor, and when I woke up I could not remember my name. Dees hospital did not know who my name was too. So you see, dees was where Mex was born. In a lot of ways, I was reborn too. Eet has stayed with me long after I remember who I was. And I never got eento a fight again," he said, shrugging his shoulders.

"What is your name then?" asked Jake."

Ole Mex just smiled and said, "Why, senor, Ole Mex, of course."

"Okay, have it your way," said Jake, smiling. "Say, you want to play a bit of cards while we wait out the storm?"

"I'm better at checkers board," said Mex, "eef you av one?"

"You bet!" said Jake, and he jumped up, putting his dishes in the sink. "I'll throw on another pot of coffee and then I'll get it. I think it's still in the pantry."

Mex went into the living room and threw another chunk of wood into the stove. Then he began to pick up his dishes and cleared the table, wiping it clean.

Jake grinned, then laughed. "You'll make some old girl a good wife someday."

Mex grinned, "Si, you are right," he said. "Just you not tell my wife about dees."

He laughed, and said "You can count on it." Jake set up the checkerboard and poured them both coffee. *It is bound to be another long, long day,* he thought, but I'm grateful for the company, and a fine one at that.

They played, chatted, and laughed the afternoon away while the wind and the snow carried on, taking everything around them to a standstill. It blew, howled and drifted, and it was cold. Yet the warmth inside was more than the kind you get from a fire. The two had found a kinship and the afternoon, well, it just drifted on.

Chapter Eighteen

Bess woke up, startled. She was in bed, her bed. Her hand carefully felt around and she realized she was alone. She breathed a sigh of relief. *I wonder what time it is?* she thought.

Bess climbed out of her bed and picked up her watch on the dresser. *Oh, my gosh, it's 12:30. How did I sleep so long?* She dressed in her blue jeans and carefully selected a blue sweatshirt. She put her feet into a pair of warm socks, slipped into her tennis shoes and crept out into the living room.

There wasn't anyone there, but the stove was warm as if it had recently been stoked up. Her kitchen was open to the living room and she peeked her head around looking to see if anyone was there. *Nope, no one*, but the coffee was on low so she reached for a cup and started to pour herself one. When she saw a cup had been placed there for her, she put the one she had away. *Then I'm not dreaming,* she thought, *all this did happen. But where*, and before she could get the words out she heard a banging at the door. It flew open and Richard was standing there grinning from ear to ear.

"Well, sleepyhead, about time you woke up."

She grinned. "Are you all right? You were so sick last night and I didn't think you would make it."

"I'm weak, but I'm okay," he said as he shut the door.

"When I went to sleep you were in the bed," she blushed, "and I was on the rocker"

"Yeah, I know," he said, smiling. "I was kind of indecent when I woke up this morning."

She was silent as he hung up his coat and took off his gloves, dusting off the snow. "But what I can't figure is how you did it all?" he said. "Sometimes you amaze me, woman."

She looked at him, speaking softly. "You do what you have to, Richard. I'm just glad you're alive."

"I see how you got me to the house last night, though. I took the sled and the blankets back out to the barn. I put the blankets on the old chest out there.

Hope that was okay, and by the way, smiley, while your peepers were closed you gave birth to a beautiful stud foal."

Her eyes lit up and she got excited. "I wanted to be there when she gave birth."

"Well, Bess, most mares like their privacy. They like to be by themselves when they give birth." He poured them both some more coffee. "Hey, I know it's late for breakfast, but how about I treat you. I'll cook!"

Bess was delighted. "That sounds good, but what about the rest of the animals? I should go feed them."

He was shaking his head, "Nope, I've taken care of everything, so you don't have to worry."

"Well, in that case, are you sure you feel up to it?"

"Yup," he said.

"What can I do to help?"

"Nothing, just you sit down and direct. Tell me where everything is, okay?

"Deal," she said.

He pan fried some bacon and eggs and toasted some of her homemade bread in the oven. He set the table and grabbed the pot of coffee, filling their cups. Then he stopped. He was quiet for a moment, his eyes searching her face, and he reached over and put his fingers in her hair. Her hand came up over the top of his. He looked into her eyes and she into his. His voice was gentle and quiet. "Thank you for saving my life, I will never be able to thank you enough."

Her eyes misted, and she said, "I couldn't have done it without the help of the old man upstairs. I was praying every step of the way."

"Let's eat," he said, "before all this gets cold." He sat down opposite of her and started telling her excitedly about the color of the colt. They talked about how they do imprint training on his ranch, and he said, "Actually, Jake knows more about it then I do, but what I do know is enough and I started your colt out with it this morning. If you have any questions, I'm sure Jake would help you any time." Then Richard changed the subject. "That was pretty ingenious thinking you did, what with the rope to the fence, then walk the fence line to the barn, then to the door. Smart move..."

"Well, actually, I don't know about ingenious, but it was the only way back and forth in this blizzard, and Rocky, he's the man of the hour. He took me to the fence last night." Then she told him her story, most of it anyway, leaving off her kisses and sliding past the part were she was naked next to him for a while. She finished by saying, "Then I guess I fell asleep in the chair."

He said, grinning. "I noticed this morning I didn't have any clothes on." Her face turned red, he smiled, he was getting a charge out of making her squirm. "Did I just dream that you were laying next to me without any clothes on, or was this just in my imagination?"

"No, Richard, you weren't imagining." Her face turning red from the embarrassment. "But you were so hypothermic and I read somewhere," she stammered, "that…that when you can't get a person to the hospital that this was the only safe way you can warm them up…" Her eyes were locked, looking down at the floor.

"I'm sorry," he said. He felt bad he hadn't intended to carry it so far. He reached over and tilted her face up, and without a second thought, he pulled her up from her chair and into his arms. He kissed her lips, she responded and, *they were so soft*, he thought, *and warm.* He kissed her eyes, her cheek, and her lips again. She moaned, a stirring arising from within. Tears were flowing from her eyes. He held her for the longest time.

The room was silent except for the ticking of the clock, the rattling wind, and the sound of the snow slapping at the window. The teakettle hummed and all else was quiet except the beating of two hearts. *This feels so right,* he thought, holding her closer. *How can I let go?* Then he spoke. "I'm sorry I don't have a right to do this. I'm so very sorry," he said as he looked into her eyes. He was reluctant to let her go. Then he pulled away and winced. Suddenly he felt stove up against his back and he groaned.

"Here," she said, "you need to sit. You've been doing too much. You're bruised and I think you have either cracked your ribs or damaged them somehow. Let's get you in the living room and you can lay down for awhile. We'll talk about this later, okay?"

He said, "Okay."

She could see all the strength had gone out of him, that he had done too much. She helped him into the living room and onto the couch. She put a pillow under his head and laid her blue quilt over him.

He said, "I'll just close my eyes for a bit." He hadn't realized how tired and exhausted he was. And before he knew it he was sound asleep.

Chapter Nineteen

When Bess thought about his kisses, her body stirred as it had never before. She felt yearnings emotionally and physically, and she was on fire. She had trouble concentrating—her mind would keep drifting back to that moment. She threw on her winter clothes and braved the storm; she wanted to see the new addition.

When she got back, Bess decided to make a quick loaf of bread so she could stay busy. While it was raising, she would peek in on Richard to see if he was okay. She knew he had done way too much. Then she cut up the chicken and put it back into the pot and set it to simmer. She made homemade noodles, slicing them and dumping them into the pot, adding a little more garlic salt. The bread was giving off a fresh baked smell all over the house and soon she was lifting it out of the oven.

Just as she was about to set it down, he spoke a whisper in her ear, "Mmmmm, that sure smells good."

She jumped, and he laughed, realizing he had surprised her.

She grinned. "You must be starving by now. Here," she motioned with her hand, "sit down and I'll dish you up a plate." He watched her as she served them both. He was amazed by her. "Would you like coffee or a glass of water? I don't have milk."

"No, coffee's fine," he said.

They both ate in silence, listening to the sounds around them, both feeling a bit awkward, each in their own thoughts.

He finally broke the silence. "This is real fine food. You're a wonderful cook."

"Thanks." She smiled. "I'm glad you like it." She thought to herself for a moment, then she said, "Richard I'm going to put you up in my room tonight. It'll be easier for you then climbing those stairs. I'll sleep upstairs in my old room."

"You don't have to do that," he said. "I can sleep up there."

"No," she said. "I wouldn't have it any other way, I insist."

"Okay, okay. I won't argue with you." He looked at her thoughtfully. "Bess, about this morning. I didn't have a right to…"

"Don't worry about it," she said quickly, lying to herself. "You were just overwhelmed and grateful, grateful to be alive."

"Ohhh," he said quietly, rolling his eyes a bit, "that might have a little to do with it, but it wasn't all of it. Bess, honesty tells me to let you in on a secret, and that is you've been getting under my skin for a long time now. It's just…" he said, pausing. She listened closely to him. "It's just that I don't feel quite right doing this to you when I'm not exactly free. Mary's gone, but I'm not really free of her and I'm sorry…I'm really very sorry."

"Don't," she said softly. "Don't apologize. It took two of us, you know, and I'm not innocent in this. I returned your kisses, you know, and I admit I enjoyed every minute of it."

"I know, I feel the same way," he said. "That's what's so darn hard, I'm sorry," he said quietly, wrinkling up his face. He stood up from his chair and yawned. "Well, I'm going to help you pick up this kitchen and then I'm going to go to bed. I'm suddenly feeling very tired." His face looked drawn and white.

"No, I want you to go on and get some sleep. Leave everything, Richard. I can handle this, I'll have it whipped out in no time."

"I believe you," he said as he smiled and headed for the bedroom. He undressed, carefully laying his clothes on the chair by the bed. He was sore and tired. His last thoughts were of the beautiful angel in the other room, and he fell into a blissful tender sleep.

Bess cleared the kitchen. When she was done she poured the water in her teakettle into her washbasin and took a short bath. She put on her nightgown and sat for a long time with the lantern low, watching the fire in her stove and listening to the night sounds. It gave her time to reflect on their conversations and his kisses earlier. She pondered all he had said. She had weighed all the facts, and even though she was frightened she had decided what it was she needed and wanted to do.

She opened up the door quietly to his room. She felt herself holding her breath, and she slipped off her gown and slid into bed next to him.

He awoke with a start. "What the? Bess?" he said quietly. He realized her bare skin was next to his. He was confused.

"Richard, I've never been with a man," she said.

It caught him off guard. He put his arms around her and pulled her close "Are you real sure this is what you want?"

"Yes, more than anything I've ever wanted in my entire life."

He held her, his body began to grow, he gently kissed her lips, her face, then he nibbled her ear. She responded in turn. She had never been so consumed with a fire such as this and so deeply in love. She knew no matter what happened she would not forget this moment and she would always love Richard. She gave of herself as she had not ever done before and the night flew by amid the wind, cold, and the snow.

Chapter Twenty

The weather was crazy. The wind was howling, snow drifting, accidents, people lost, and the sheriff was tired. It had been a hair over two days of snow blowing and just downright nasty weather. His only consolation prize had been his newfound relationship with Sarah. She belonged to the high society page and somehow didn't fit into his idea of a relationship, because in the past Sarah ran with Mary, and that in itself spelled trouble.

He had thought a lot about them both, and Sarah was a lot different than Mary. Mary did a lot of partying, and unknown to Rich she was well known for screwing anything she could get her claws into. She preferred money, *because money talks you know,* he thought, *but Mary wasn't beyond messing with men without money either, as long as they were good looking.* The sheriff tried to steer clear of her as best he could. She was hard to resist, this he knew, but besides that, there was the fact he really didn't want to tangle with Rich.

He remembered the time he saw him double up his fist and deck Sam. Now Sam had had it coming to him, the sheriff had no doubt, but that didn't stop him from wondering what Sam must have felt like when he woke up. Rich, to his way of thinking, was a powerful, powerful man who managed to keep in shape simply by working hard on his ranch.

There was only one time that he'd let himself be talked into meeting Mary and he had regretted it ever since. Mary didn't forget these things and it caused him to worry him every time she showed up, that he might get caught in it. Mary wasn't beyond telling about her escapades when it suited her, or when it caused others great harm.

Yesterday when Jeff had picked up the phone and dialed Sarah's number he thought when she answered she was real nervous, especially when he said he was coming by to pick her up, her voice was a near panic. She wanted to meet him somewhere and he said a flat no. There was a silence, then she snapped loudly, "FINE! Come by if that's what you really want to do!"

"What is the matter with you?" he said. "You know this storm is so bad that I really don't want you out in it. Doesn't that make sense to you?"

"Whatever," she said quietly.

"Fine," he said, "I'll see you in ten." When he arrived at her home, she greeted him at the door.

"I want some answers, Sarah. Why were you so snarly, and why don't you want me picking you up here?" he asked, hanging his coat and hat up.

Just then a voice he knew spoke up. "Because of me," said Mary seductively.

He turned around and looked at her. He was surprised, "How long have you been here?" he asked, then he got angry, "Do you know what kind of a commotion you have caused this whole damn town. Rich, your husband, and not to mention your folks who have been worried sick about you?"

"Yeah, don't ya just love it?" she said, smiling. "Rich, he deserved it after hitting me, and as for Deanie and Wess, they'll survive."

Sarah was getting shook; this was not what she wanted. She was falling in love with Jeff and she didn't want Mary anywhere near him. She really hadn't wanted him to know she had given Mary a place to stay, or that she had any part in hiding her.

The sheriff sat there shaking his head, and asked, "Sarah, are you ready to go?"

"No, I'm not. I'm sorry," she said quietly. "Would you mind waiting a few more minutes? I wasn't prepared for you to pick me up, I needed a little more time."

"Sure," he said, he felt uneasy though. Sarah left the room and Mary coolly walked over and put her hand under his shirt. He grabbed her hand, looking around to see where Sarah was, hoping she hadn't seen. "Stop it," he said.

She raised her eyebrows and grinned. "What's the matter you, afraid she'll catch you? Boy, could I tell her some stories," she said as she jerked her hand away from him.

He grabbed her again, this time harder and he pulled her back. "You keep your flippin' damn mouth shut. You understand me?"

"Or what?" she said. "You'll what—run to Rich and tattle? I hardly think so."

Jeff looked at her and just shook his head, "It's no wonder Rich belted you. A little of you goes a long ways, honey."

"You fuckin' asshole," she said. "What I could do to you!"

"Shut up," he said. "You want Sarah to hear you?"

"Ask me if I give a fuck? Go ahead, ask me."

The sheriff smiled and said, "You know something, Rich told me when you left you had a filthy mouth—he was right about you."

That infuriated her. "YOU better watch your back, Jeff. Nobody, but nobody puts one over on me. YOU hear me?" she said, "NOBODY," as she stormed off.

"I'm real worried—see the worried look on my face," he had told her. He was glad when he and Sarah finally got out of her house and left for a while. But Jeff knew, thinking back about that whole scene from last night, well…he really was worried, and he sat in his office and mulled all this over in his mind.

Sarah wasn't like her, she was soft and gentle and kind. Even though he had money it didn't seem to make any difference to her. She seemed to be content to spend time just sitting in his house and talking by the hour. He knew she had pursued him, but that was okay. He had been lonesome far to long. He liked the fact she was considerate with others, which proved to him there was more to her than meets the eye, and reality was checking in. He knew he was falling in love with Sarah. *This*, he said to himself, *is a scary deal, I haven't told her how I feel.* Then he thought, *To make matters worse this morning, who should call me but Mary and gives the code word Lady from Redding.* He thought, *I about crapped when she called. She had set that up once, just once, when I decided to taste that delicious morsel, or so I thought at the time, And now it's all coming back to haunt me, smack in my face. I hope like hell Rich never finds out about us or he'll kill her and me both. I told her not to ever call here again she screamed at me telling me that she demanded to see me and I had better jump right now and meet with her or she was going to holler at the top of her lungs to Rich and Sarah that we had been together. Damn her,* he thought. *How am I going to get out of this one?* He told her it would have to wait until the weather cleared up, that right now his plate was full. He'd call her when he was more free. He thought this might give him more time to think of something in the meantime. He knew she wouldn't wait long. He was getting a headache. *Maybe, I need to eat,* he thought. *I know I'm hungry,* so he got up from his chair and headed out his door.

"Bob, I'm going to head out to the Double A Café. I'm hungry, so I'll be gone awhile. If you need me, or anything important comes up, you can reach me there."

"Okay," said Bob. "You look real tired anyway."

"Yeah, I am," he said as his fingers tapped lightly on the desk. "If," he said quietly, "if I've been out of sorts these last two days I apologize. There's been so much going on and I haven't had any decent sleep since it all began."

"I know," said Bob, grinning. "I only called you an old crab once."

This made Jeff grin. "Thanks, and you too, Mr. Loveable."

Bob just smiled

Jeff headed out the door, only to quickly turn and put on his heavier jacket. The gusts of wind were so strong he fought to stand upright. He turned the key, unlocking his pickup door and sat down, closing the door behind him. He sat there for a few minutes and then called dispatch letting them know where he was. He still sat there thinking about Mary, and it kept going over and over in his mind how he was going to handle this thing with her. *I could kill her,* he thought. *I could do it so no one would ever find out, and Rich would be better off, this much I know.* He warmed his rig up and waited. She could have an accident, that wouldn't be too hard to arrange. Then his thought turned to Sarah. *Would she ever forgive me if I did that? For that matter will she ever forgive me for what I've done? Hmmmm now that I think about it, that tip we got the day Mary supposedly disappeared was from a woman. She knew an awful lot about the whole situation. I 'd bet you a dollar to a donut or anything it was Mary, trying to get Rich into trouble, and she damn near did manage it.*

He put the truck into gear and looking both ways, he backed out. He had put the truck into four-wheel drive at the beginning of this storm and had left it there. He thought about Rich and where he might be by now, remembering Jake's phone call. He was supposed to call me back if he didn't hear from him. But then, Jeff surmised, he probably couldn't, the phone lines have been out. He pulled into the café and called dispatch again to let them know he had arrived.

Jeff hurried in and shut the door. *Good,* he thought, *George Simmons is here. I'll ask him how long before the phones are up.*

Kathy smiled when he came in. She was in her favorite corner with George. Jeff decided to join him.

"Hey, George, mind if I join you?" he said

George laughed as he looked up and said, "Do I have a choice?"

"NO," laughed Jeff, and he sat down. "Kathy, I'll have my usual, please."

"Sorry, Jeff, but believe it or not, we're out of chicken fried steaks. Ed's running a special on beef tips over noodles, green beans, and a hot roll, coffee included."

"Now that sounds real good. I'll have that, thanks."

Kathy wrote the ticket and then brought him coffee. She made herself scarce. It looked like a business meeting to her and she didn't want to butt in.

"George?" he said half loudly…

George looked up. "Hmm, I knew this was serious."

"No, not that serious, at least not yet, anyway. This here's my problem. Yesterday Jake Reed over at the Gannon ranch called me. He was concerned that Rich Gannon hadn't shown up yet that afternoon—it was the beginning of this storm."

Kathy was at their side. She set Jeff's dinner down in front of him and poured them both another fill of coffee. "Thanks, Kathy…"

"You're welcome, Sheriff," she said and left.

"Anyway, as I was saying, it was at the beginning of this storm and I told him not to sweat about it, that I'm sure he got in somewhere, but now I'm not really sure that he did and I'm a bit worried. He was going to call me if he didn't hear from him, but then with all the phone lines being down he couldn't call me if he wanted to."

"Yeah, I heard Jake was looking for him." George thought for a moment, "Well, it's like this, the only help I can give you is what information I have on hand at this moment. We have the lines up and working right up to his neighbor Bess Cramer, but we still don't have them working to the Gannon place, not just yet anyway. You have to remember we can do only what we can do and especially in this weather. We're not only fighting the weather, but to get to the lines and get them working it's a real bitch. The lines, they keep snapping and the wire is stiff. I'm about to pull my hair out."

"No, that's fine," he said. "Maybe I'll give the Cramer place a ring," he said, contemplating," I'll try that first, and if she hasn't heard from him I may have to take a drive out to the Gannon ranch, even if I have to get a snowplow to clear the way." He took another drink of his coffee. "For some reason this is really bugging me. I guess I've been so busy with everything else it just didn't occur to me this might be serious."

"Too much going on, Jeff," George said, shaking his head

Then the two got off onto another subject and ate and talked and then they had dessert. When the check came, Jeff insisted he get it. "After all," he said, "you let me pick your brain and I interrupted your meal. It's only fair I pick up the tab."

"Well, thanks, you can interrupt anytime." He grinned.

Jeff paid and George reached into his pocket and lifted out a hefty bill and set it on the table for Kathy. Jeff grinned and nudged him. "Wouldn't it be cheaper just to get hitched to her? After all, I hear through the vine she's just plumb nuts about you."

George said, "She doesn't know it, but when this weather breaks I'm purposing to her. And she will never have to work another day in her natural life. It's a two way street, you know," he said as he tipped his head sideways. "I'm just as crazy about her."

They bundled up warm against the mean cold outside. Jeff knew he was on a mission, so he wasted no time getting into his truck. Once again he radioed dispatch to let them know he was warming up his truck, he was finished with his meal.

When the sheriff got back, he had a phone call waiting for him. This made him uneasy until Bob told him it was Sam. He was sure Mary was going to call any minute.

"Hey, Sam, how are you?"

"I'm a lot better thanks to you. This was the best thing you could have done for me. I didn't realize I was on such an explosive trail."

"Hey, it's okay, buddy. I'm glad that you are doing better. Say, when will you get to come home, not that you would want to today? We've had a storm, the worst we have seen in a long time."

"Well, as soon as that nasty storm you have going up there is through, I would like very much to come home," said Sam quietly.

"Are you ready?" he asked.

"Yes, I have passed all the battery of tests with one-hundred percent and my temper is under control. And I owe you an apology, Jeff."

"I don't want you thinking that. You did the right thing by taking the anger management program," he said.

"Say, Jeff, will I still have a job? I mean, I know I left under real bad circumstances. Will there be a job for me when I return?"

"You bet you will," said Jeff. "You know Rich didn't want to press charges and that really was all that was left standing in your way, except getting your temper under control. And it sounds as if you done just that. So I guess you will be showing up as soon as this weather clears?"

"You bet," he said. His voice was excited. "I'm thankful. Really, really thankful, that he didn't press charges. It could have been real bad for me."

"Rich is a good man, Sam, but I'm glad for you too. Well, I hope it clears real soon, you know I could have used you during all this." Jeff laughed.

"Well, I guess there's always next year, isn't there? Well, I have to go, Jeff. I'll see you soon."

"Sure thing. Have a good one," and he hung up the phone. Jeff knew that Sam had gotten off light. When Mary did her disappearing act, Jeff remembered Rich was brought in for questioning. Sam had been told to come cool off back at the station. He was still mad at Rich for decking him. When he arrived back at the station, he was sporting a fight. When Rich was hauled into the interrogation room, the detectives hadn't returned from his place. *I went to get me a cup of coffee and found myself answering questions about what had happened by our local paper The Examiner. This, unfortunately, left him all alone in the room with the doors closed. I wasn't privy to their conversations, all I knew was that all of a sudden I heard big a commotion. I remember jumping up and running through the door and there was Sam beating the crap out of Rich who still had one handcuff attached to the chair. Before he could stop the whole thing, Rich had Sam flipped on the ground (God I remember how strong he was) and he was delivering punch after punch until I pulled them apart,* Jeff thought. *Actually it took three of us to get Rich off him. That's why,* he told himself and he felt a chill go up his back, *I can't let Mary stir up shit. Why oh why did I let myself get talked into having a fling with her? It was short but not so sweet.*

Jeff's phone light was blinking. He picked it up—it was Bob. "Yes, Bob, what's up?"

"Well, you have Sarah on line two and the lady from Redding on line three."

"SHIT!" said Jeff

"What did you say, Sheriff?"

"Ahh, nothing. Listen, would you tell Sarah I'll call her right back, that I'm tied up for the moment and patch me through to Miss Redding!"

"Sure thing," said Bob

Jeff sat there for a few seconds trying to get his composure. He took a deep breath and punched line three. "Yes, what do you want? And why are you calling me here? I'm busy."

"That's no way to talk to a lady," Mary said smugly

"Since when did you become a lady?" he asked.

"Oh, come now, don't be such a sore ass," she said coyly

"Can't you ever talk without that filth coming out of your mouth, Mary? I mean, for crap's sake, I don't even talk like that. You sound like a trucker sometimes."

"Ahhhh, poor, poor baby you don't like my potty mouth."

Jeff was getting tired of dealing with her, and he didn't want play her games any more. "What is it you want?" he said impatiently

"I want you to meet me somewhere. I want you to fill my fire. There, was that nice enough?"

Jeff felt sick inside. "I'm not going to meet you," he said quietly. "You know darn good and well I'm dating Sarah and I know that fact really bugs you, but that's too bad."

"You bastard," she said quietly. "What would you think if I told Sarah you dipped your wick into my candle? For that matter, I could tell her a lot of naughty things about you that aren't true."

"Mary, come on you really think that scares me? She wouldn't believe you."

"Yes, it does. It scares the hell out of you," she said. "She's been my best friend since childhood. Yeah, she would believe me, you can bet on it."

He changed the subject. "What else is stirring up with you, trouble?"

"Well I did have another thing I wanted to ask about while I have you on the line. I want to know the scuttlebutt on Rich. After all, we are still married. He didn't get into trouble when I left like I had hoped he would."

"Yeah, too bad for you, wasn't it?" he said quietly. "Not much to tell, and I wouldn't even say this if you weren't still married to him, except that Jake seems to think he's missing out there in the snow somewhere. He called me yesterday worried about him. Rich didn't show up at the ranch and the storm was and is still in full force. Other than that, nothing, but if there was any other kind of juice I wouldn't tell you about it anyway."

"Hmmm, lost in a storm. Maybe I'll get his money after all and the ranch with very little trouble. Hmmm, no courts. This could get very interesting. That's all I need for now, but I'll be calling you back, so don't get too comfy."

"I wish you wouldn't, I could do without that," said Jeff, clearly irritated. "I'm tired of all this," and he slammed the phone down in her ear.

Jeff felt exhausted. It had been another long day and he still had two more phone calls to make. He decided to return Sarah's call for now and Bess's phone call could wait until morning. It was late and he would place it then. He wondered if the world ever got better, or if life just kept stabbing at you as you went. *Sometimes,* he thought, *well, just sometimes.*

Chapter Twenty-One

He opened his eyes and quietly laid there watching her, touching her face as she slept. His whole being felt a sense of wonderment, and for the first time he new a completeness. Never had he ever experienced this kind of a feeling before. His heart swelled, she had given so much and asks so little, and he knew he wanted to spend the rest of his life with her. He had taken her carefully and tenderly, and he knew she had spoken the truth; she hadn't ever been with a man before. *She's so special,* he thought. He felt the chill in the house and he knew he needed to get up and build the fire and yet he was so mesmerized by her. It made it difficult, he was reluctant to move from her.

The cold won out, and so he carefully removed his arm from under her body and slipped out to the stove. He had shut the door so she would sleep. Richard balled up several pieces of paper, teepeed the sticks of kindling and set pieces of wood on top. He struck his match and torched it off. Just then the phone rang. Startled, he quickly picked it up so as not to wake her.

"Hello," he said quietly. "Yes, Sheriff, I'm okay. No, I rolled my truck. Yeah, I'm kind of stuck here for now. She did? When? I'll find out about more of the details later," he said as he rubbed the back of his neck. "Yeah, I'm real lucky to be alive. Uh-huh, Bess saved my life. I would have frozen to death if she hadn't found me. County trucks...oh! Okay! No, this is the first the phone has rung. He was? Yeah, would you mind...let him know I'm okay and just as soon as it lets up I'll be home. Thanks, Sheriff, bye."

Richard reached down and unplugged the phone. He didn't want to talk to Jake just now, or anyone else for that matter. He was comfortable right where he was. He took two steaming cups of coffee into the bedroom and set one down on the chair beside Bess. He put his arm around her and snuggled in.

"Thought I dreamed all this," she whispered. "I was so sure of it and I didn't want to wake up." The tears were quietly falling from her eyes.

He pulled her close and said, "No, beautiful...this wasn't a dream." He closed his arms around her tighter and kissed her softly. They laid there, each in their own thoughts. He felt the reality of the whole situation and knew he was going to have to deal with his wife. That is if he could find where she had kegged up. *Well,* he thought, *I'll take care of that later.*

"That coffee smells so good," she said as she reached her hand out and took a sip. "Was that the phone I heard, or was I dreaming earlier."

"No, the phones aren't on yet," he lied. *Why did I tell her that?* he thought. *Maybe because, like her, I don't want this to end. I don't want to share her with anyone, I love her so much it hurts.* He pulled her close, holding her tight. His eyes swelled up a bit, he was feeling all these strange new emotions. He had never experienced feelings this deep before—she overwhelmed him. He turned her over, brushing the hair from her eyes and pulled her into his arms again and gently kissed her face, searching her eyes.

She looked at him and saw the deep passion, his love, it was all revealed in his face and the gentleness of his body next to hers. For the first time in her life she felt safe, wanted, and deeply loved.

The fire crackled, warming the house, and old man winter laughed outside. The dog and cat snuggled next to the fire and all was quiet, but for the world within was one of one body and one mind and no one…not even winter was invited in.

Chapter Twenty-Two

Most of the day, after the chores had been done, was spent in each other's arms. They held each other like there was no tomorrow, and in reality for them there was not. They avoided talking about Mary. It was much easier to deal with. But he happily spoke about his kids, and it was clear to see he was crazy about them. Bess saw in him the good father he was. He laughed about the good times and drew silent about the sad times, but he always spoke with pride.

"Bess, let's hear more about you," he said, holding her even closer.

"What do you want to hear? There really isn't very much to tell," she said.

"Well, is Bess your real name? And here goes the big one." He turned her face to his and spoke gently.

"What?" she said, searching his eyes.

"How come you have never been with a man before? I mean, it's not a bad thing. It's just that you really took me by surprise considering your age and the times nowadays. It isn't fashionable to wait. I don't know," he was feeling embarrassed, "I was really blown away. It was like having the greatest gift given to you all wrapped up in a beautiful package with a pretty bow tied to it."

She sat silent for a minute, then she said, "When I was growing up, my dad always told me how special it was, and how precious a gift it would be some day to the man of my dreams. I guess I just held out because it didn't feel right. And the right person didn't come along until now. I had plenty offers along the way, and a lot of stupid remarks," she said, laughing. "Like if you loved me, you would show it. I'm a man, honey, I need to release these things. I'm not like you. And on and on and on, you know how it is. Well, maybe you don't, but anyway, I guess I…well, I just never bit into the logic that I needed to give it over. It meant more to me than that. It was like my dad said, it's special and it makes you even more special, not even to mention the fact it is against all that God has in his plans for you. I'm not a perfect human being, and I believe God watches out for those that love him even when they step over the line. I knew someday when it was right that I would give everything I had to give to the one I love, and I did." Then she said, "I'm not ashamed, nor do I regret what I've done. You see, Richard, this moment may be all I have and I wanted it to be beautiful. Ours. Belonging to no one but you and me. No one can take that from me. I'll put it in my picture book of memories."

He sat there quiet for the longest time. "Bess, I can't promise you the moon now." Shaking his head, he was feeling sick, "I don't have it to promise you."

"Shh," she said quietly. "I didn't ask you for the moon."

"I know you didn't, but I want to give it to you in ways you have never known before."

"Richard, I don't know what the future holds. But right here and right now is what I want and I'm not asking for anything more."

"I know," he said. "THAT's the trouble, I want more for you. I'll be leaving soon and I hesitate to even think about it."

"Then don't," she said, smiling. "Now the name thing you asked me about. My name it is actually Bethleen and Bess for short. When I was little, Dad started calling me Bess and I guess it stuck."

"That's a beautiful name. How come you don't use it now that you're all grown up?"

"Oh, it was just easier to keep the Bess, and I got used to it and too hard to explain to everyone why I would like the other better."

"Now for the big one. Why is it you call me Richard when everyone else calls me Rich? Now mind you, I like it, I like it just fine. It doesn't bother me at all, somehow sounds so right coming from your lips."

She smiled. "Richard," she whispered…rolling the name quietly off her lips. "Richard is a full, strong, but warm and gentle name. It says I'm bright…it's formal and yet it's not. Richard is a loving name. It sounds like love. Nothing taken from it, nothing shortened to make it less, or you less, and it fits this unique wonderful loving individual who I love with all my heart. I couldn't give of myself to a Rich. It takes away from you," she said. "But a Richard is…is full of that moon you spoke about, and why not have the moon?" she asked.

"You overwhelm me. I'm flattered," he said, shaking his head. "I really don't know what to say." Then a thought came to his mind. "Would you mind if I call you Bethleen? It's beautiful, you know."

"No, I wouldn't mind," she said. "I'd like that very much. The wind sounds like it's letting up out there." She got up and looked out the window and pulled the curtain back. "Snow isn't coming down now, that's a good sign."

"Not really," he said as he stood behind her. He reached his arms around her, touching her hair, holding her. He rested his chin on top her head and closed his eyes. "As soon as it lets up I have to go," he said ever so quietly, "and I'm not ready to do that."

Bess turned to him, her eyes stinging from her tears.

"Ohh, it will be alright, little one," he said gently. "Don't cry. We'll figure this thing out even if it means I can't see you for a while. Don't give up on me. I know I haven't said it before, but only because I don't take it lightly, I love you more than life itself," he said as he held her face in his hands. "I'll find a way if it's the last thing I do, and by the way, I didn't tell you before because I didn't want this to end, but the phone lines are up and I unplugged the phone. I'm sorry, but I wanted this to last and I didn't want anyone to interfere with you and me."

"It's okay," she said blowing her nose. "No big deal. So who was on the phone?"

"It was the sheriff. I guess Jake has been worried and called them. Only the phone lines aren't up at our place yet and until they do Jake won't know I'm okay. Anyway, the sheriff said even though they can't legally come into people's driveway to clear them out, it's a big no-no, the town had decided that since this was the worst storm they have had in years they'll be sending the trucks around to clear everyone out. Bethleen, they are sending one in here in the morning," he said quietly.

"It had to happen sooner or later, Richard. I guess it's just reality, life you know."

"Bethleen, I want to talk to you about when I leave."

"You don't have to now," she said.

"Yes, I do, and then it's done and we won't speak of it again. We will spend the rest of our time together holding on to each other. When I go, I have a lot of things to do. I've made a decision not to contact you." He saw her wince. "Not because I don't want to. It will be hard, ohhh so damn hard," he said as he shook his head, "but because I love you, Bethleen," he pulled her even closer, he didn't want to look into her eyes, "I was also told when the sheriff called that Mary has produced a miracle and she alive and kicking."

"How?" she gasped.

"I don't know the details, I don't really care at this moment, and it really doesn't matter, not now anyway. But I do want to protect you in every way I can. Mary is what they call a bad seed. She will make you pay in ways you would never believe, someone that evil. And I don't want you exposed to that. Just remember I'll be working to get this mess straightened out for the both of us. Remember. Remember, that I love you so much and don't give up hope, don't give up on me, okay?" he said as he looked into her eyes.

"I promise," she said.

As the day progressed, the wind let up more and the snow had ceased. Bess made a bargain with herself not think about tomorrow. It was as if it didn't exist in her mind. She was going to savor every moment she had with him. They talked about her dad and how hard he had been on her, and about a mom she never knew who had run away. She told him how bitter her dad seemed to be about women in general. "That they love you and leave you." He had told her many times, but her dad had a soft side to him.

She would catch him looking at her funny sometimes, and would ask, "What's the matter?" He'd say, "Oh, I was just thinking of who you remind me of and how odd it is—never mind," he'd say, and then he'd wander off.

"It was the oddest thing he did the day before he died. He had left a long message on my answering machine, and that was unusual in itself, but what he said didn't make a lot of sense. He started by saying he needed to talk to me. That it was very important. He needed me to call him or come see him soon. Then his voice softened, and he said, 'I love you, child. You have always been my own. And now you are my own, don't you forget that. I love you deeply. Call me soon, and if you don't get this in time, look in the box. Love your, Dad.' It was like getting a letter from him. I didn't get that message in time to see him. He died that night and I never got a chance to ask him what his message was all about. It has confused me ever since, it left unanswered questions, and it's strange, so very strange."

"Have you looked through everything he left behind?" asked Richard.

"No," she said. "I still have boxes in the attic and I seem to keep avoiding them. It's just too hard to look in them. Maybe one of these days I will be able too, but not now."

Their day had been full and they had shared so much, it was as if they were packing a lifetime into a few stolen hours. He picked her up into his arms and kissed her passionately. "I love you," he whispered.

She closed her eyes and loved him back. He gently kicked the door to the bedroom open and shut it with his boot, taking her into a world full of love and passion.

Chapter Twenty-Three

When Rich arrived at the ranch house, Jake and the old Mexican were out in the barn. The sun had come out peeking on occasion, out from under the clouds. Snow was piled in drifts here and there left from the storm, but it had warmed up and things were beginning to melt. When Rich took a look in the barn he could see Jake repairing a saddle and ole Mex was rolling up a hundred feet of rope or so. They both spotted him at the same time, their eyes bright and warm with welcome.

"How did you get here?" he grinned, holding his hand out to shake it. Then he grabbed him in a bear hug.

Rich grabbed his hand and embraced him. Laughing, he said, "I hitched a ride with a county truck."

"Damn, I glad to see you," he said. "Sit down. Sit down!" his voice was excited. "I want to hear about everything."

The old Mexican crossed himself, saying a silent prayer, "Dees Heavenly Father he has beeen good to you, yes? Welcome home, senor," he said, reaching his hand out.

Rich shook his hand. "Thanks, it's good to know I was missed," he said, smiling.

Jake said, "Well, I wouldn't go so far as to say you were missed." Then he laughed. His face got serious and he said, "It is good to have you home, son."

"The feeling's mutual, Jake"

They talked for what seemed like hours. He filled them in on almost all of the details of his ordeal. Finally he slapped his knee lightly and got up. "Well," he said, "enough of wasting this day. I'm going to head up to the house, I've got to call the kids and sometime today I need a shower and to get cleaned up, so I'll see you later."

"Not me," said ole Mex. "I promise dee ole woman I be home soon."

"Okay then, Jake, I guess it's just you and me." Then thinking out loud to himself, he muttered, "I'll see you after a bit."

Jake quipped with, "I have plenty here to keep me busy for a while. See you later when you're done."

74

Rich shook his head, and shutting the barn door behind him, his thoughts once again returned to Bethleen. He doubled up his fist and slapped it into his open hand. "I've got to stop doing this," he said aloud. "I need to concentrate on the problems at hand."

Chapter Twenty-Four

When Rich left the ranch, he left without telling Jake anything. He had a lot on his mind and he was on a mission. His decision to divorce Mary was an easy one. Getting it done, though, that might take some doing, but he knew one of the best lawyers in town, and that in itself made him feel better. He needed to shop sometime for an older Chevy pick up since he had rolled his. Jake didn't know he had taken his rig to town, but he was sure that he wouldn't mind.

God, he thought, *I miss her. I hate being away. Even one minute is too long from her. I wonder what she's doing now?*. Then his thoughts turned to Jake. *He didn't ask, but I saw in his eyes the questions, questions he would have liked to of asked.* Then she came to his mind again and for him this was an ache that wouldn't go away, he wanted to be close to her. He wanted to smell her hair, touch her body, wake up next to her and watch her sleep. He wished there was a way to get rid of Mary faster. *That would suit me just fine*, he thought.

Then, speak of the devil, there she was big as life, right in my face, he thought, shaking his head, *taking my parking space*. He felt a tightness in his chest as he pulled in with Jake's truck behind her and stepped out his door.

"Well, I heard you decided to come back to living," he said, smiling.

"Too bad you just didn't just die out there, asshole, then I could have it all," she said smugly, her head just dancing, for she was on a roll. "You can bet I'd sell everything on that stupid ranch, then you know what I'd do? I'd fire that asshole Jake, boot his fucking ass off that place so quick he'd never know what happened to him and walk away from this God forsaken rathole."

"Phew," he said, "your nasty mouth is really running this morning, isn't it?"

She didn't answer. She just glared at him.

"It's nice of you to be so concerned about me. So you would have liked it if I had died out there?" he said. "Well, it wasn't in the cards, sweetheart." He contemplated for a moment, then he said, "Someone out there said a prayer for me I'm sure."

"I'm sure you would like to think it was your precious sweet Bess," said Mary with a snotty whine in her voice. "I heard you stayed with her for three days. Bet you played more than spin the bottle."

"Now there's a thought," he said, grinning as he raised his eyebrows. "Thanks for the suggestion."

"Go to hell," she said, angry. "I don't plan on leaving you with anything anyway, not even a pot to piss in."

"You never were a lady anyway. Too bad you didn't just stay gone," said Rich.

"I wish they would have put you in jail, that would have suited me just fine," she said.

"Why did you come back?" asked Rich in a quiet voice.

"Because I want your money. I want everything you own, you hear, everything you own."

He grabbed her hard by the arm and got real close to her face. She looked scared, and he said in a low terrifying whisper, "Don't bet on it, honey." With that Rich walked away.

He left her standing on the sidewalk with her mouth gaping open and headed down the street, stepping into Bailey and Bailey Attorney At Law.

Jeanie looked up and smiled. "Hi, what can we help you with today, Mr. Gannon?"

"Well, I was hoping John was in today, and if he is, could I get in to see him?"

"He is," she said, "but right now he with a client. He has an opening in about forty-five minutes. Would you like me to set that up for you?"

"Yes, I would," he said. "This is real important."

"Would you like a cup of coffee while you wait, Mr. Gannon?"

"No," said Rich, "I'm going to walk down to the Double A Café, I'll be back in time. Okay?"

"Okay," said Jeanie, nodding her head, "see you then."

He walked out, letting out a big sigh. He still felt the anger boiling inside of him and knew the walk would do him some good. He put his hands into his pockets, and then as he walked down the street, he felt the cold wind chill him clear to his bones. That's when he decided to zip up his jacket and pull his hat tighter on his head. He thought about Bess and the last few days, his love for her, the laughter they shared, and all she meant to him. But for now he would have to table those thoughts, for he had a lot on his mind and still a lot to do.

He noticed the snow was being cleared from the middle of the street, the aftermath of the big storm. There was still some slush on the sidewalks and the roads. Shivering, he walked into the warmth of the café. Taking his hat and coat off, he sat down on a stool away from the main door. Kathy quickly noticed him and headed his way.

She smiled at him and said, "Menu or just coffee this morning?"

"Just coffee, Kathy, thanks," said Rich.

"I heard about your ordeal," she said. "You look pretty good for someone who almost died."

"Do I look ghost-like?" He smiled.

"No, of course not. I just meant, well, you know what I meant, don't you, Rich?"

"Yes, I know what you mean," he said." But you want to know something—I don't think I'll ever get warm again. I heard you guys were really hopping in here for those three days."

Kathy smiled in understanding. "Yes, it was," she said as she rolled her eyes, "and I can't even imagine what it was like for you to be that cold, and frankly I don't EVER want to find out." She poured Rich a little more coffee, then she saw George come in and everyone knew she was sweet on George. She took off right away, but not before she said, "I'll be back with more coffee in a bit okay, Rich?"

"Sure," he said, smiling to himself.

A few minutes later a couple of friends of his sat down at the bar, and Kathy handed them a menu and poured them a cup of coffee. They were headed for the auction yard and had decided to stop and get breakfast. They talked about cows, prices, and water in the coming spring. They wanted to know the details about his experience and between refills of coffee he told his story.

Time passed quickly, and before he knew it he had about five minutes until his appointment. He put his hand over his cup and told Kathy he'd had enough, that he was expected elsewhere. Rich lay down money for his coffee and an extra couple of bucks for her tip.

She smiled and said, "Thanks."

He grinned back and said, "Anytime," as he put on his jacket and hat, and bundled up to go out the door. Heading up the street, he again felt the cold chill on his back and hurried himself along.

Opening the door to John Bailey's office, Jeanie, the secretary, looked up and said, "Mr. Gannon, he'll be right with you. He's still with another client."

"Okay, thanks, and please call me Rich, Mr. Gannon was my Dad."

"Sure Mr. ah…err, I mean, Rich."

"Hey, that already sounds better," he said, smiling.

Just then the door to John's office opened and out stepped Mrs. Clemens the third. He thought to himself, *She must be getting on eighty years old by now and quite the lady at that.*

She smiled at Rich and reached out her hand, switching the cane. "Hi, young man, I hear you were staring ole man winter in the eye," she said warmly.

"That's right," he said, "and I spit right back in his face."

"You're lucky," she said with mist in her eyes, "not many live after spitting in his face. Besides, I kind of think the Lord likes you or you wouldn't be here."

"Somehow I believe you, Mrs. Clemens," he said softly, "Someone WAS watching out over me, otherwise I'd have never made it out of that storm."

She gripped his hand and gave it a squeeze. Then she turned to John, "You'll have my papers done up and ready to sign this next week?"

"Yes, ma'am, I'll have Jeanie give you a call when they are ready."

"Thanksm John, and young fellow," she said as she turned to Rich, "you take good care of yourself." As she closed the door, Rich nodded his head and touched the brim of his hat in agreement. Realizing he had put his hat back on when Mrs. Clemons had left, he again took it off and reached to shake John's hand.

John took his hand and said, "What can we do for you today?"

"Well," said Rich stroking his chin.

John knew this looked serious. "Come on in," he said and closed the door behind them.

Chapter Twenty-Five

An hour later Rich stepped out of Bailey and Bailey and got into the pickup truck and headed back home to the ranch. The highways were still mucky and full of slush, making it hard to steer the truck. It was as if the wheels had a mind of their own. Snow plows were everywhere trying to clear the roads from three days of storm. Some places were still not passable, and it made it slow going in some areas. The sky was clouded over and a mist was in the air like it thought about dropping more snow, or perhaps rain. When he pulled into the driveway to the ranch, he felt his body was drained, as if he'd been up a full twenty-four hours working a fence line. Rich was tired.

He opened the back door to the house and stepped into the kitchen. Jake was pouring himself a cup of coffee. Reaching into the cupboard, he grabbed another cup and poured Rich one too. He said nothing as Rich walked in, but with his eyebrow raised, he had a look that said where have you been.

Rich sighed, his smile was grim, but he decided now was as good a time as any to tell Jake they may have to sell part of the ranch to buy out Mary. He told him only what was necessary to tell about what he had talked about to John at the attorney's office. He said it didn't look good, even though she was the one who tried to fake her own death. Then he decided to tell him about the conversation he had with Mary on the street. He could see Jake's face getting redder by the minute.

He said, "You know what? She didn't once ask about how the kids were. All she thought about was how she could get all the money from me. How do you tell your kids that their mom could care less about them?" Then he answered his own question, "I guess you don't."

Jake was boiling. "I don't know how you stood there and took it so long. I would of knocked the lights out of that bitch right there and then on the street."

"No you wouldn't, Jake," said Rich. "You're a lot of talk, bud, but in the long run you'd of just gave her a mouth full of cuss."

"Bullshit," said Jake

"Bullshit yourself. Just let it go. It's not worth tearing your stomach up over, she's not worth it."

"What I want to know is this," said Jake. "WHY?"

"Why did I get mixed up with her?"

"Yes, why did you get mixed up with her in the first place? There's nothing inside, she's empty. Why, she don't even like the likes of her own. Those two kids are great and they don't even know what a mother is, let alone their mother. All she ever cared about was herself and high society and keeping herself in the limelight. As long as she was in the limelight, she was happy."

"Slow down, partner," said Rich as he looked out his kitchen window. "I know you're pissed, but blowing up is not going to solve this problem. We need to put our heads together and see what kind of solution we can come up with."

Jake sat there quiet for a long time with a troubled look on his face. Finally he got up. Putting his cup in the sink, he walked to the door. "Don't worry," he said with a small grin. "I might have a way out."

Then he shut the door behind him and headed out toward the barn.

Rich sat there rubbing his forehead and finally put his head into his hands. He closed his eyes and Bess came to mind. He felt a stirring in him he had never felt with any other woman, not even Mary. He couldn't seem to get his mind off her and he knew he'd better keep to the business at hand or Mary was going to stir up more trouble. Then he thought about the night in the snowstorm when he was with her, and how he had felt safe and warm inside. *Oh, if only life could be so good,* he thought. *Why does it have to be so damn complicated and miserable? Why did he get mixed up with the likes of Mary, couldn't he see what she was?* He knew the answer, of course. He was just trying to do the right thing, she said she was pregnant. He was foolish and old fashioned then. He believed it and he believed he could make a go of it, that in time things would change, if he would only stick it out long enough. Truth be known, they only got worse for them both. The arguments escalated and became more bitter between them as the days wore on, causing them both to hate one another with a ferocious passion. This did nothing for their kids' frame of mind; it only served to teach them how a rotten marriage can be. That reminded him he needed to phone them.

Rich reached for the phone and dialed the number. "Hi," he said, "how are you guys doing?"

Wess said, "Good as can be expected and ya? I heard that ya were in sum big snowstorm."

"Yeah, I was, I'm lucky to be alive really."

"That's what I heah," he said,

"Can I talk to the kids a minute? Then I want a moment with the both of you, okay?"

"Shurah...TYLOR...Kayleen...it's yor Papa on the phone."

"Hi, Dad!" they said in unison.

"Hi, kids! Are you having fun with Grandma and Grandpa?"

"Yes, but when will we get to come home, though, Dad," asked Tylor

"Well, I'm going to have to leave you there a few more weeks until Daddy gets a few things straightened out, okay?"

"Okay, but I would rather be with you," said Kayleen.

"I know, but it can't be helped right now. You'll see, sweetheart. Time will fly and before you know it you will be home with me. I love you both. Now let me talk to your grandparents, okay?"

"We love you too, Daddy."

"I'll call you soon, all right?"

"Okay," said the kids.

Then Wess and Deanie both picked up the phone and Deanie spoke first. She said, "What's up, Rich?"

"I wanted to be the one to let you know Mary is alive and she's in town." He heard a gasp on the line. "I don't know the details as yet, where she was or what she was doing," he said, "but we managed to scream at one another again, and on the street," he said, sighing. "Somehow, it seems so hard for us to be nice to one another. Anyway, I wanted to be the one to tell the kids, but in person if I could."

"Sure," said Deanie quietly.

"If she should show up there and see them all hell could break loose. I really didn't want them exposed to this, not this way anyway. All I'm asking is, please don't let her take off with the kids. I know she's your daughter, but it wouldn't be very good for them. This is too much for the kids to understand and I think you will agree. I just want to be the one to break it to them. This would mean a lot to me."

Deanie, who was always very outspoken said, "I honestly didn't think she had gone too far. I was sure in my mind Mary was just hiding out somewhere, and don't ask me why I felt that way, cause I really don't know. Anyway, don't you worry your head about such matters, she may be our daughter, but she's been a lousy mother and I would, as you know, tell her that to her face. There's no way I'll let her get a hold of these kids."

"Thanks, Deanie," said Rich. "I appreciate that. For now I'd like to keep the kids at your place, if you wouldn't mind just a little longer. I think they would be better off with you while I have a chance to sort out this whole mess."

"That's no problem is it, Wess?" said Deanie

"No," he said quietly, "no problem at all."

"You know, Rich, sometimes I think they switched my kid at birth," said Deanie sadly. "She sure doesn't act like she came from me."

Rich had to stifle a small giggle. "Anyway, I'll call you and let you know what's going on at this end," and with that they all said their goodbyes.

He thought to himself how lucky he had been to have these folks as in-laws. And with that thought in mind he headed out the door to give Jake a hand.

Chapter Twenty-Six

Mary had taken on airs even as a small child. She knew her folks had plenty of money. They lived on a large ranch of fifteen-thousand acres or more, a lot of desert, but most good fertile land that held two stables of sorts that housed fifty or so high bred horses. The house was not a home. It was a southern mansion that had so many bedrooms that you couldn't count on your two hands and feet. It was definitely large. She tolerated her folks, but she really didn't like them. She felt her dad was a weenie and drank too much, and her mom was this loud and overbearing goat. Though not true, this was how she perceived them in her mind. They were only a convenience, someone who could provide for her plenty of money and prestige. She had no conscience when it came to using them for whatever she needed. She seemed to be born without any knowledge of right or wrong, and lacked feelings for others. At any rate, they were an embarrassment to her. They had sent her to the best schools to educate her, hoping she would find some sort of compassion or feeling along the way. It proved to be their undoing. It had given her a sense of the taste of life she fully intended to keep. She promised herself she would never be poor, and to party was the grace of life. Mary had become very self important. She wasn't past lying or cheating to get what she wanted. The only real pleasure she felt in life was spreading her legs and horseback riding, and then she was down right mean when it came to both animals.

Mary was an only child and had grown up with plenty of servants to wait on her. She kept them in their place at all times. After all, she was the princess of the mansion. Her parents worried that perhaps they had done way too much for her and knew that she managed to wrap them around her fingers, but she was the only child that Clydean and Wesley were able to have. That it made it hard not to indulge her. The ranch was self-supporting, each field containing corn, wheat, oats, and rye. It had a grove of apple trees, walnut trees, and one or two berry fields. There were cattle on one section of the ranch and small housing in another; a cookhouse and bunkhouse were not far from the stables. They employed about fifty-three hands and most of them had families. Deanie ran a hard, but fair hand over it all. The arrangement suited Wess just fine. It gave him more time to indulge in sipping his afternoon tea—of sorts.

Mary's thoughts on life were simple. Everything and everyone should bend to her needs, her feelings, her whims, her thoughts, and definitely her beauty. She was certainly a strikingly beautiful woman. She knew from childhood she was special. With all the ohhh's and ahhhh's as she would get as she entered her mother's circle of friends. Her blonde hair was long and flowing and she was about five foot five with the slender build of a New York model. Heads would always turn when she walked through the door. She secretly would smile to herself and throw an extra sway to her hips. Her favorite pastime was social parties, any event that would have allowed her to make her entrance, and certainly to be the center of it all. Mary loved to party. She never missed a social event.

Sitting in her car after her heated argument with Rich, she was still shaking. Not just from being angry though, but because she had never seen him so furious. Thinking back to when she first met him, she remembered the very party that she had attended, the social event of the season. That is what had started this whole thing, and she wouldn't have dreamed of missing Mrs. Clemens annual spring event. Where Rich Gannon came into being. Everyone who was considered anyone or to be prominent, the upper crust so to speak, was invited. To get the opportunity to rub elbows with this crowd was a special honor. Everyone who was anyone or was important would be there. Mary arrived in the red sports car that was given to her on her last birthday. The attendant helped her from her car and she happily handed him her keys. She was dressed in one of her favorite outfits, a tank dress that was white with tiny red flowers. It flowed loosely at the waist and fell to just above her knees. Around her neck drooped a small gold heart trimmed in diamonds. Mrs. Clemens the third had out done herself, everything was set up out in her beautiful gardens in the back. She had the tables covered with linens; colorful umbrellas and flowers everywhere. It was breathtaking to take in; she had outdone herself and as if she had set it up herself, the weather was lovely and warm. Croquet was set up in one corner of the garden and horseshoes in the other. The guests were milling about talking, drinking, and some playing games. All the ranchers small and large were always invited to the affair. It was her way of welcoming in the spring, and it was only fitting everyone should join her.

Mary spotted Rich Gannon and leaned into her friend Sarah, whispering, "Who is that? He's so good looking, and why haven't I seen him before?"

Sarah smiled, "THAT, my dear, is Mr. Rich Gannon and you haven't seen him before because he does not EVER come to these shindigs. You've been off to school and abroad, that's why he is new to you. Besides, he's out of your league. And, honey, he doesn't circulate in your social circle."

"Oh, I don't know about that," she said. "Has he got any money, and is he married, Sarah?"

"Why, yes, my dear, he's loaded, self made, and no, he's not attached, but darlin' he won't like the likes of you. I hear he's more for the homespun type. You know, the kind that likes to make bread and babies and such, and that doesn't include you.

Mary smiled. "Don't bet on it. There's more than one way to catch a fish. Besides, you just offered me a challenge and I like a good challenge."

She slowly wandered over his way, making small talk with everyone on the way. She watched the way he handled himself with those around him, the way he laughed, his physique. Mary was like a cat and he was her prey. She watched how he held himself, was careful not to be observed. He was too busy pitching horseshoes, laughing and drinking to notice her approaching, but all the other men turned their heads as soon as she headed their direction. They admired her packaging and drooled to themselves. She was clearly irritated that he did not turn around when all the other men had seen her and nodded their heads. She spoke to him, and it wasn't in a very pleasant tone. "Most men are gentleman and acknowledge a lady when she presents herself in their company."

Rich looked up and smiled. Taking his hat off, he said, " It clearly was not my intention to offend the lady, and I beg her pardon. I only ask that she kindly forgive me."

She smiled and reached out her hand. "I would like to introduce myself. I'm Mary Harlow, Wess and Clydean's daughter. For that matter, their only daughter," she said as she laughed to herself. "You must be Rich Gannon, I presume?" she said like she didn't already know who he was.

"Yes, I am, ma'am. Glad to make your acquaintance."

"Could I buy you a drink?" she said, smiling.

He hesitated, and then he offered his arm and looked over at the men saying, "Excuse me, gentlemen, I believe the lady as given me an offer I can't refuse."

Mary smiled inwardly to herself. She had won and the plan had formed in her mind. No one, after all, no one ever walks away from the goddess Mary, and it was her observation he had hesitated when she tried to seduce him to leave with her. She had decided right then and there he was the catch she wanted. Not that she cared about him, and he didn't know it, but she had plans in mind, marriage plans. *You don't turn me down,* she thought, and she was not about to let him get away as they climbed into her car and drove away.

Mary thought about all this as she sat there in her car contemplating her future. She remembered the night she had left and he was blamed for her disappearance. This made her smile wickedly. They had gotten into a screaming match, and as usual she had pushed it too far, only this time Rich blew and she wasn't expecting that. He hit her and bloodied her nose and broke open her lip. *He was sorry, oh so sorry he said,* she thought sarcastically. Mary remembered being furious and frustrated. She had found a towel and wiped her lip when he left, laying back on her bed, her face stinging from the blow. That's when the plan formed in her mind. She began running through the house dumping everything she could get her hands on. *She would leave,* she had told herself, *and take only as little as needed.* She dumped most of her clothes on the floor. Taking a couple of things, she threw them over her arm. Mary reached for her special bracelet behind the jewelry box, knocking it off and scattering its contents all over the floor. Then she had felt under her mattress, retrieving the money she had stashed there for some time. She remembered thinking to herself, *You poor stupid idiot. you didn't even know I took your money.* From there Mary had headed downstairs, scattering everything she could get her hands on. Heading for the kitchen, she had went to the freezer and pulled out the tray. Her nose and mouth hurt and she needed to get the swelling down. When it wouldn't pop open, Mary took a knife and tried to pry it out in the sink. It slipped, cutting her finger. She was bleeding all over the place. Mary had wrapped it in a piece of towel paper. She screamed, stomping her foot, "This is enough! I've had enough! I'm out of here." Walking out the door leaving it open, she dripped blood all the way down the walk and through the gate. She had started to latch it when a car pulled up. "No, thinking back," she said aloud. *I really don't care what he did or didn't do any more it doesn't concern me now except for the money. And I don't give a damn about those brats. I really didn't want them anyway,* she thought. *And somehow he's going to pay for hitting me. I've had enough of playing games, the part of housewife and mother I had played is over, and over now. I'm done.* "No more," she said aloud as she turned the key on her ignition and drove off. "No more."

Chapter Twenty-Seven

It had been almost a week since Richard had gone from Bess's place, when Jake pulled up in his pickup truck. She was glad to see him.

"Hi, Peaches," he said, when she opened the door.

"Hi, Jake, come on in, how you doing?"

"Good, good, and you?" he said

"Would you like some coffee? I just made a fresh pot and it just now finished perking."

"Sure, I'd like that," he said. He sat down at her table. While Bess busied herself at the stove, Jake took a look around her place. It was neat and clean. *Her kitchen isn't very big,* he thought. *It's narrow, her dad must have built it on.* It looked like a tunnel to him, and at the end of it was her sink and just above that was a window. The cupboards weren't fancy and needed paint. For whatever reason, they had been painted green in spots. Her counters had the old-fashioned linoleum on them and metal trim. Her stove was in a small section all to itself and it was old, but then it had been her dad's. All this looked into the dining room that was a step down, and Bess had an old wooden oblong table that needed resanding and a fix.

"Thanks," he said when she handed him his coffee. "Say, when your dad added this room, why did he put in so many windowpanes?"

She looked at them and said, "Actually, this was part of the original old house, it was the section in the kitchen that has all the cupboards that he put in...Bess walked over to the window, touching one of the panes, she felt of it fondly. "Would you like to hear a story about this windowpane? It's one on my dad and me," she said as she pulled up a chair,."It makes me laugh every time I think about it."

"Sure, I'm all ears," he said.

"Well, when I was fifteen years old."

"And that was a long, long time ago," he laughed

"Jaaake! Come on. You want to hear this or not?" She smiled, rolling her eyes.

"Okay. I promise to behave," he said as he patted her hand.

"Anyway, as I said, I was a girl of fifteen and I had decided I was going to make my dad a Father's Day dinner that coming Sunday. Every morning as I rushed out the door heading for school, I would remind him to take the chicken out of our freezer for Sunday dinner...he would nod his head, of course, and say uh-huh. Well, I was a typical kid. By the time I would get home with chores and schoolwork and things I would forget about it. Well, this went on for a couple of days and then I just plum forgot about it altogether. Come Sunday morning we went to church and when we got back my dad went to go feed the animals. I was all excited I rushed in the house and looked in the fridge for my chicken. No chicken, not anywhere. Here it is his special chicken dinner and I don't know where it is. Then it dawned on me maybe he never took it out of the freezer in the first place. Hmmm, bingo it was still in there. Well, I want you to know that really ticked me off, and don't forget I was just a kid. I screamed, 'How in heck am I suppose to make Father's Day dinner if the stupid chicken is still frozen!' I said a no no word, son of a bitch! I screamed, I was so mad and I threw it on the floor, Jake did you know that a frozen chicken would bounce?"

Jake shook his head no, but he was laughing by now.

Bess grinned. "Well, it does," she said, pouring them some more coffee. "It bounced so hard from here, flying past this stove, and it ricocheted clear in here through this dining room over the table," and then she pointed, "out this very pane. And it landed at my dad's feet. My dad said very quietly to himself and I could hear him, 'Boy I don't know if I want to go in there or not.' I started to laugh and I laughed so hard the tears were rolling down my cheeks."

"I bet your dad got a charge out of that," said Jake.

"Yes, he did," she said, "and he took me in to a Father's Day meal at the café, and when he got back home he went out to the barn and found another pane and fixed it right up. And you know, he never once said anything about that no-no word that came out of my mouth. Now when I look at this pane of glass I think of him and it reminds me of that funny story and I smile."

"You miss him, don't you?" he said.

"Yeah, Jake, sometimes it gets so lonely for me here. I mean, I don't miss the city, not at all. But I'm hungry to have someone of my own, someone who belongs only to me." She felt her eyes mist up and she thought of Richard and it hurt.

Jake reached across the table and touched her hand. "I know, Peaches," he said, "but sometimes in life we have to wait, and when it's right, and when that special someone comes along you will know. It will be right only with them. You know, there are a lot of folks out there," he about thought of Rich and Mary, "who just pretend to be happy. They aren't in love and they get married anyway, or for the wrong reasons. Then they stand back and hurt one another for the rest of their lives, never knowin' how special a good love can be. Your dad wouldn't want that kind of a marriage for you. It's better you wait until it's right and it's someone you can't ever do without."

"I know," she said, "but sometimes all the good ones are taken."

"I've heard that before," said Jake, and he grinned. "You have someone in mind?"

She felt alarmed. "No, no Jake," she said, shaking her head. "Just speculating that's all, I was about to go out and check on my new addition. You want to come?"

"Sure," he said. "Rich told me about him, said he was real pretty."

"I need some tips, I've never done this before. Every day, though, I spend, or try to spend, at least two hours with him."

"That's good," said Jake as he got up. He laid his hand on her shoulder. "Bess, there are two reasons I came by to see you today. I wanted to know if you were okay. Your dad once made me promise to watch out over you if anything ever happened to him and I take my job seriously."

She smiled. "I know you do and, yes, I'm fine."

"I wonder though, sometimes if you would tell me if things weren't fine," he said.

She grinned. "You know me pretty good, but if it's real serious, Jake, I promise I'll be at your door."

"That's what I wanted to hear. Now for the other reason I'm here."

"Oh boy, now what did I do?" she said, smiling

"Well, as a matter of fact, IT IS what you did."

"What?" she said, her brow curled up in a frown.

"Oh, Peaches, it's not bad. Rich didn't tell me any of the details except he was frozen half to death. He said he would be dead if it weren't for you. I just wanted to thank you." He put his arms around her and pulled her to his chest. "Thank you for saving his life."

"Jake, you don't have to thank me. I would have done it for anyone."

"I know," he said, "but thanks anyway. Now say, how about you show me that new youngin' of yours."

She slipped into her hat and coat and opened the door. It felt in a way like her dad was still alive. *It feels good to have company,* she thought. *I didn't realize how lonesome I am.* As she stepped out the door, they both admired the skiff of green peeking out through the patch of snow on the ground.

"It'll be spring soon," he said.

"Yeah, I could do with a bit of spring," she said, and she closed the door.

For Bess the days were slow. It was an effort for her to even get a handle on the days sometimes. She decided maybe she had better look into her cupboards. It had been awhile since she had done any shopping. There wasn't much of anything in them and she knew the hour was late, but chose to go anyway. She closed the door and headed for town. It was the still moments that brought him to her. The times she couldn't control her thoughts. She would find the stirring in her as intense as when he first touched her. It felt as if her skin was on fire and she would burn. Just the thought of him, of his touch. And she traced her finger on her face.

Bess turned her wipers up to full, the rain had begun to pour, rat-tattering on the roof of her pickup truck. When she pulled into town, it was a quarter past ten. *It's awful late to be shopping,* she thought when she looked at her watch. She slammed the door shut and stuck the keys into her pocket. When she looked up, his laughter echoed in the rain. He was talking to another person who was coming out the door. He didn't see her. It felt like her heart had stopped, she couldn't move and the rain was soaking her clothes. He got into the pickup started it up and drove off. She just stood there, she was sick. She thought, *I don't think I can deal with this, Lord.* Her tears flowed with the rain. Her hair was dripping and she couldn't seem to move. "I can't take this, Lord," she whispered. "Please, please, please," she begged. "Make this right for me. I don't have the strength to go on. I love him so much and my heart hurts, it hurts real bad." She sobbed. She got back into her pickup, she had lost her appetite, not only for food, but she no longer had the desire to shop. She turned the key, heading home and the rain fell.

The night turned into days and days into nights. It had been more difficult for Bess then she had anticipated and she had cried every night after he had left. The days were filled with his emptiness and the house did not seem the same. She wrote in her journal on a daily basis now, and the pages were filled with her love for him.

She wrote:

Richard, this I know to be true, until you came into my life it was not complete; I did not come to know love…I have felt this way from the very moment I first set my eyes on you, and it was troubling because you belong to another. I feel a sense of passion in me that has awakened that I did not know existed before. This fire you have left in my body reaches out like a thirst that needs to be quenched, it has touched my very soul…you came for but a moment in my life and that's not enough… for you are and always will be my true soul mate of this I'm sure…I don't know the why of it, we have missed one another along the way. Or if in time we truly will hold each other until all time. I only know you have affected me in ways that no one has been before you. You are in my heart in places no one has ever touched, or has ever been able to touch, in my soul…it leaves me drained of the very essence of life, for without you I do not exist. You spoke of putting my thoughts on paper, that the things I write should be written, but without you these things have no meaning and without you my life seems at an end…I love you more passionately than anything I have ever loved in my life…I love you, Richard…to speak your name draws breath from my soul…and I cannot breathe. I cannot breathe with out you…I love you.

Bess then set down to fill her page with a poem she had written through a mist of tears.

In my book I can be with thee
To reread the passages of time
To feel you close in my dreams
For just that moment you'll be mine

The tears I've shed since you have been gone
Fills the rivers that run near by
The aching that you left in my soul
Makes me question the why

I often hide among the pages
Looking for the answers in my mind
The wondering why we can't be together
My love for thee in kind

Bess closed her book. The rain had been falling, it tittered and tattered on the old roof of the house. It wasn't a comfort to her as it had been in the past. It only gave way to her sadness, making her feel more alone in this world. She thought of him and ached for his arms around her. Her memories all she could hold. She would play them over and over in her mind hanging on to the very thread of them, for these thoughts were her own. The what if's plagued her until she was almost physically ill. She found herself eating only because she had to, nothing tasted good. She had become way to thin and knew it. Her heart was broken and even though he said not to give up, she was slowly believing he was gone. The light was ebbing out of her eyes. It was all she could manage to push herself out of the bed in the morning and do her daily things. "If he would only just give me one jingle," she said. "One sign he still cares." *There I go again,* she said. *If only...if only.*

Chapter Twenty-Eight

The aching in Rich's heart kept him awake most nights, and it stirred in his mind throughout the day. He wished that the days would fly into the nights and the nights into days. If this were at all possible, then perhaps it would bring him closer to being with Bethleen. When he dreamed at night, it was fretful. He would toss and turn, then get up, pace the floor and go back and toss and turn. His dreams were his saving grace, for in them he held this gentle angel, this woman with the big blue eyes. If only he had the magic at his fingertips perhaps he could wish her to him.

In the days, Rich would pretend that all was okay, when in truth it was not.

Jake kept asking him if he was all right. "You sure?" he said, "You seem more quiet, like something eating away at you."

"Yeah, Jake, I'm fine, just fine. Let it go, will ya!"

Jake decided maybe the storm had taken it out of him. Perhaps being that close to death changes a man. All Jake knew was that he was a lot more silent and moody. Rich had always been a hard worker, but Jake took note he was putting his back into the ranch work with a fury, as if death had gripped him. It was as if he was possessed and needed to rid himself of this demon, throwing his sweat into it and causing pure exhaustion. For the most part he ignored Jake and went about his own way. But for Rich this was the time he could hold to his memory of the storm and of his love for a beautiful woman.

He had asked John, his lawyer, to speed up his divorce. He said I'll give it all if I have to I just want OUT of this marriage. It had been bad from the start. When she got the divorce papers Mary had been furious. Rich had been repairing the picket fence by the house when he heard the wheels of her car squeal to a stop. Mary jumped out and her face was beet red. Rich laid the hammer down and spit the nail out of his mouth.

"What brings you out slumming?" he said.

She screamed at him, "What the hell makes you think I'll give you one?" Then she threw the divorce papers on the ground in front of him.

"You will," he said calmly, picking them up he threw them back in her car, and he said, "By the way, since you don't give a hoot about our kids I want them too." His fingers carefully traced the hammer's handle. *It would be so easy to pick this up and do away with her right now*, he thought. *God, I hate this woman.* His jaw tightened and he felt his teeth clench.

"What if I told you I'm going to take your precious little ones away?" she said smugly. "That I'll fight you on this?"

"You won't and I can guarantee it, cause," he said, deadly quiet. "you don't have a leg to stand on, Mary. When the court gets a hold of your records…well, let's see," he said lifting his eyebrows, "parties—lots of them. Ahhh and let's see YOU left the kids, abandoned them and me, not even a word of your whereabouts, not to anyone, and that's including your parents. You stole twelve-thousand dollars from the ranch account, and, oh by the way, what about all the men you have opened your legs for since we've been married? Nope, I don't think so."

Her eyes got real big and she was surprised. She stammered, "That, that money was mine and I never…"

"Ohhh," he said smiling, "you look surprised. You didn't know that I knew, did you? Well, girl, men talk, and BOY do they talk. You'll find most of them aren't gentlemen. I should have put you out of your misery a long time ago. I should have taken my gun out and disposed of you, gotten rid of your body, dug a big hole, it would be so easy you know." He picked up a nail in his hand and pointed to it. "I have a bullet with your name on it," he said. Then he touched it to her forehead.

"You son of a bitch," she said. "You bastard, you wouldn't dare. You don't have the guts."

Quietly steeling his lips he tapped his finger hard on her chest, "Trust me, sweetheart, push me too far. Go ahead, I dare you. Just you go ahead and push me. It would give me great pleasure to do you in."

Chapter Twenty-Nine

It had been a month almost to the day, and true to his word she had not seen or heard from Richard. She had woke up this morning feeling like she had the flu, only her body wasn't aching and she didn't seem to have any fever. She had puked all morning long and didn't try to eat anything for breakfast. She felt like crap and had thought perhaps if she took Teco out for a ride that the fresh air would do her some good.

When she got back, Bess was not feeling a whole lot better, but decided that at least her chores were done and she might lay down for awhile. She was taking off his blankets when she heard a noise behind her. Bess caught her breath in her throat when she turned around and a fist came up and struck her in the stomach, then one to her face. She didn't have time to realize what was going on. She fell and doubled up in pain, her eyes closed.

Then she heard a growl. Bess was looking straight into Mary's eyes and Rocky was by the door threatening to bite Mary. She screamed, "You stupid dog!" and he growled again. He sounded mean and this startled her. She had never heard this sound from him before. Her voice raspy, she quietly said to the dog, "No, Rocky."

"I want you to know," said Mary hotly, "I think you screwed my old man when you had him here with you during that storm."

Bess didn't answer, she was in too much pain. She staggered, pulling herself up. She was still winded and her eye hurt. Then she said, "Mary, please, just go. Leave me alone."

Mary looked like she could kill her. Then she spouted, "Listen to me, bitch, nobody, but nobody touches what is mine. Remember this," she said as she put her hands on her hips. "YOU talk to him, YOU go near him YOU so much as touch him, I'll kill you, bitch, but I'll do your dog in first. And you won't hear it coming," she said. As she pushed Bess to the ground, Rocky growled as he lunged for her.

Bess screamed, "No!" and the dog stopped short of Mary as she backed out of the barn. She lay there on the ground for close to an hour feeling like she was going to die. Finally she pulled herself up and got into her pickup. She knew this was bad, she had never been this sick before. Her stomach hurt and she was cramping and it felt like crap. She got her keys and slid into the pickup and headed to the hospital. She didn't feel well at all.

Her doctor was on call and took her right away. "You're kind of white in the face, young lady," he said. "Tell me what happened. Who hit you?" He began touching her face, looking into her eyes and examining the bruise on her jaw.

Bess told him about Mary, she told him what she had said and how she had struck her from behind and in the face.

"You know I'll have to inform the sheriff. It's my job, but right now I want to take some tests on you. You've lost a lot of weight since I've seen you last and I will want to see what's going on with you. So," he said, "you thought you had the flu this morning, but no fever and you're cramping now?"

"Yes, doctor. I puked all morning long. I just didn't have any of the other symptoms."

"Well, we'll take those tests," he said, "just to be on the safe side. I'll need to get a urine sample as well and take blood pressure, and when we get all done, I'll meet you in my office. In the meantime I want you to get into this gown. I want to take a pap, you're overdue and we'll do an exam while we are there. Okay?"

"Sure," she said. Bess undressed. It had been some time since she had been examined. *Oh, I feel awful,* she thought, *and weak.*

When he had completed the exam, he said, "Get dressed and I'll see you around the corner."

She sat in his office and looked around while she waited. She noticed his picture of his wife and kids on his desk and the books that were displayed on his shelves. His room was neat, and it was pleasant to sit there.

Just then he opened the door and sat down in his chair. Wheeling it over to her, he took her hand.

Bess felt a sense of panic and thought in her mind this must be bad. He said softly, "Do you want to tell me about it?"

"What?" she said with a question on her face.

"Bess, hon, I'm not sure how to put this to you but straight out. You're pregnant."

She gasped, "But how? I mean, I never thought, I didn't know. Oh, my gosh!" and she started crying.

"Bess, listen to me, Bess," he said, "When Mary hit you, well, let me put it this way. If we aren't careful right now and because of your age and all the other factors you could easily lose this baby."

The words stung. "Oh no, I, I…" She was sobbing.

"Bess, I want to put you in the hospital. I want you to be very careful right now. We can admit you this minute. Claria can do the paperwork."

"No, doctor I can't," she said quickly. "No, I have to go home. There's no one to take care of my animals and I don't want anyone to know. Not yet anyway."

"I don't know about this," he said, then giving some thought to it, he said, "Okay, we'll do this then. I'm going to give you these pills. I want you to take them twice a day. If you need more, just call my office and ask to speak directly to me. If they give you trouble, just tell them you were instructed to do so. Now I want you to go home and get off your feet. I want them up and elevated for a few days. Find someone to do the animals for you, no heavy lifting for you, young lady. Complete bed rest for at least a week. Bess, are you listening to me?"

She nodded her head yes.

"Bess are you okay?"

"Yes, doctor, I'll be okay, I just wasn't expecting this. I just didn't, I didn't," and she began to cry again. The loudspeaker rang out above her head as she walked slowly out of his office.

"Doctor Cannon emergency room four."

"Doctor Cannon emergency room four, code blue."

Dr Bingham was worried about Bess. He felt sorry for her. He turned to the nurse on duty and gently grabbed her arm, "I don't want one word breathed about this, do you understand?"

"Yes, doctor," she said.

Bess was in slow motion, crying when she saw Jake at the end of the hall. He put his arms around her and she felt safe like her dad was standing there.

"Mary had no right to do this to you," he said. "You look awful, Peaches. I'm taking you to Sally's."

She looked at him and said, "How did you know what she did?"

"Well, it like this—she came bragging to Rich about what she had done to you. He didn't want to cause you a scene so he sent me down to bring you to him."

Bess pulled away. She started sobbing again, this time they caught in her throat and she wasn't able to speak very clear. "Jake, I can't cause him any, any trouble. He can't know."

Jake said, "He does know, sugar. He knows all about what she did."

"NNNO, Jake, you don't understand," she said. "Jake, I'm, I'm going to, to, oh," she let out a big sigh, "My God!" she said, his face was frowning, not understanding.

"What, hon? It will be all right."

She was shaking her head no. "Jake, I'm going to have Richard's baby. I. I…ahhhhh," she sobbed as she put her hand over her mouth.

"Oh, my God, what has he gotten you into?" he said. He thought, *Shit what a mess this is.* He took her into his arms and told her, "Hush, little one, all the more reason you need to see Rich right now. You have to tell him. Come on now, get into my truck, I'm taking you there right now," and he opened the door and lifted her in. On the drive there he questioned her about what the doctor had to say. She told him everything, and finally he said, "Well, don't you worry, there will be plenty of hands to take care of your place until you are up and about."

Jake and Bess pulled into Sally's place and he turned off the motor, reached his hand over and took hers. "Bess, I promise you Rich will make this right with you, but I want a few minutes alone with him, though, okay?"

She nodded her head. "Okay, Jake."

He thought, *She sounds so weak,* and took note that she'd lost a lot of weight. He opened her door and helped her out of his pickup. Putting an arm around her, he took her into Sally's living room. Sally and Rich greeted them.

Jake said, "I want to talk to you in the kitchen!" Rich's eyes looked at him, it was a what now look.

"Okay," he said with a worried expression on his face.

Sally took Bess into her living room and laid her on her couch, putting a pillow under her head and a blanket over her shoulders. She sat with her while the men talked in whispers in the kitchen.

Jake sat down and said, "Rich, if it weren't for the women in there I'd punch your lights out."

"Why?" He looked puzzled. "Because Mary hit her? I'd like to punch her lights too."

Jake said, "No, you asshole, because she's pregnant and you're responsible. It's your baby she's carrying, and you haven't bothered to look in on her in almost a month. Don't you see how tiny she's become? Why, there's almost nothing to her."

Rich sat down. He was floored—he was stunned. "A baby? My God, I didn't dream…I didn't think…"

"That right, you didn't think. That girl is white as a sheet and it's a real possibility she could lose this baby. And I'd like to kick your asshole clear up to your shoulder blades." Jake was mad and Rich knew it.

Rich was looked down at his feet. He seemed lost in this new thought. He thought about all this information. He felt like killing Mary and he was overwhelmed with the news about his baby. He hadn't thought to protect her. It had just never occurred to him. He had been so consumed with his love for her that the thought had never entered his mind.

"Jake, I honestly didn't mean for this to happen to her. I fell in love with her and it just happened."

"It doesn't matter how it happened now, it happened," said Jake. "Now what are you going to do to make it right?"

"I will. I promise I will make it right with her, and not because I have to, but because I want to. I love her, don't you see?"

"You go in there and you tell her that. Let her know she's not alone in this. You know, she didn't want me to tell you? She wanted me to take her right home. Didn't want to trouble you, said you had enough going on."

"Now why doesn't that surprise me," sighed Rich.

Rich got up from his chair and went into Sally's living room. He sat down by Bess and took her hand. Her face was bruised and she looked a mess. *He was right,* he thought, *she is white as a sheet. I have to make this right.*

"How you doing?" he said to Bess.

Her eyes were sleepy and her face was in pain from more than just the bruise on her face. She looked at him and began to cry. "I'm sorry, so sorry," she said.

"Oh, Bethleen, it will be all right," he said.

"You don't understand, Richard," she said, "I have to tell you something."

"I know," he said, "Jake told me, so don't you go worrying about it."

"I didn't mean for this to happen," she sobbed. "You have enough…"

"Don't worry, please, this is more my fault than yours and, besides, I want this baby and I want you," he said quietly as he held her hand with both of his. "I'll take care of you both, and I'm going to take care of Mary too. She's going to pay for this one way or another."

"No, Richard, don't, she was just defending what's hers."

"That's just like you, Bethleen, thinking of her. She doesn't deserve it. You know it and I don't belong to her anymore anyway, only on paper and that won't be much longer. Jake tells me you need to stay down for a few days, so this is what we'll do. I want you to stay at Sally's for a few days and we are

100

going to take care of things at your ranch. I want you to sleep, keep your feet up, and rest. I don't want to lose you or the baby, I want you well. I love you, Bethleen." Then he took her into his arms and held her, caressing her hair. She was softly crying. "Don't you worry, darlin'," he said, "everything is going to be all right."

His voice was soothing to her and before she knew it she was sound asleep. He sat there next to her. He ached for her, this should not have ever happened. He thought about Mary. *She is the cruelest person I have ever known. Bethleen does not deserve this. I'm glad,* he thought to himself, *about this baby of ours. I like kids and now I'll have one with the one person in my life I love more deeply than anyone I know. A baby,* he thought as he rolled it over and over in his mind. *Wow!* and then he yelled in his mind, *YES YES!*

Then a thought struck him, *We have to keep this from Mary. We can't let her find out, not for now anyway. She will do her best to destroy Bethleen and the baby, and I won't let it happen. I need to watch her around the clock so she can't hurt her.*

Chapter Thirty

Jake and Sally sat in the kitchen at her old table. Sally wasn't sure what was going on and she waited for Jake to look up and explain things to her. He looked worried, and she knew it was serious. She thought to herself, *Bess looks real sick.* She was very pale. She thought, *Hmmmm, almost as if she were...that's it!* she thought. *She's carrying Rich's baby. Oh, my God, what a mess.* Finally, after what seemed hours, Jake spoke.

"Sally, I'm sorry you are sitting here in the dark and the last to know. I don't know exactly how to break this to you, so I'll just tell you like it is, Bess is carrying Rich's baby." She sat there still and patiently listened. "She didn't find this out until just this morning, and that was after Mary came into her barn and beat the living hell out of her."

"Oh no!" said Sally.

"Yes, well, it gets worse. Rich didn't know anything about it either till just a few minutes ago, and from all that she has told me, there's a possibility she could lose this baby. Doc says she's way too thin. She's lost so much weight in this last month, and I'm going to say it's safe to assume that it's from pining over Rich. To my knowledge, he hasn't contacted her since he left after the storm. I will again assume that it was to keep Mary from doing exactly what she did. Then Mary came to the ranch this morning, found her in the barn and proceeded to beat the living hell out of her. It didn't do the baby any good, or her for that matter. This just didn't help her situation any. He wants her off her feet. She's only to get up to go to the bathroom. He wants her feet elevated, and he gave her some pills to take. She didn't want to stay in the hospital, and maybe with Mary prowling around it would be better for the moment. We need to keep an eye on her. What I want to know is, can I count on you to let her stay here for a while? I know it would to be extra work for you."

Sally took Jake's hand, "Jake Reed, I love that girl as much as you do, and I'm proud that you would ask for my help. But you must know, you don't even have to ask, that it would be fine. Now how about you and I sneaking off to the café and letting these kids be to themselves for awhile? I imagine they have a lot to talk about."

Jake grabbed her around her waist and said for the first time ever, "It's no wonder I love you so much."

Sally pulled back with a surprised look on her face.

"Hey, don't look so startled," he said. "It came to me in a dream and I finally realized I don't want to live my life, whatever time I have left, without you."

She smiled, "You know how long I've waited to hear you say those words?"

"Yeah," he said smiling, "and I've watched as you've muscled all those other ladies that tried to get within two feet of me."

"Come on, I wasn't that bad. Was I?"

"Yes, you were, but I kind of liked it," he said, grinning. "Come on," he said, "let's get out of here. Let's eat and we can talk about our plans."

"Jake, before we go I have one thing I want to say to you. Rich is a good man, he'll do right by that little gal. He's had a good teacher all these years, and it wasn't his dad, it was you."

"Thanks, Sal. I appreciate that," he said.

Sally smiled at him. "Now about that dream you said you had…"

Chapter Thirty-One

Jake and Sally enjoyed the meal they had ordered and talked about what their future would be like. They made plans for the summer. This was when Sally wanted to tie the knot, and it was perfectly suitable for Jake. He was game for whatever she had in mind. He felt a sense of relief that it was out in the open now. Both of them decided to pick out the ring together. Not because she didn't trust him, but because he wanted her to be happy with it. Sally had a glow now in her face that she didn't sport before. It wasn't so much that her love was greater or less, it was that he had finally popped the question, and she could now openly say to the world, this man really loves me, and he chose me. They finally got back to the subject of Rich and Bess.

"I wonder what they were talking about," said Jake. "I wonder how all this is going to turn out."

She looked at him compassionately, "It's going to be fine, Jake. You have to trust them to work it out. He's a fine man and I have a feeling he'll make it good. Besides, I plan to pin him to the wall."

Jake looked up from his plate, his eyebrows raised and saw the mischievous smile on her face. He smiled now. "I'll just bet you will," he said. When they finished with their lunch, Jake said, "As much as I would like to lollygag all day with you, I have to get back. We all have decisions to make and work to do and this isn't getting them done."

"You're right," she said.

Jake hollered at Kathy for his ticket. He left a nice tip for her and paid the bill. He opened the door for Sally and escorted her out to the pickup.

Soon they were turning into Sally's. When they walked back into the house it was quiet. Bess was sleeping and Rich was sitting on the floor beside her, running his fingers through her hair. He reached a finger to his lips to let them know she was asleep and whispered, "Shhhhh" quietly. They came in as quietly as they could. Jake motioned for Rich to follow him into Sally's kitchen.

Jake said, "I'd like to talk to you about, ah, what we can do to help her, if you don't mind?"

"No, that's fine, I think we need to plan this out," he said, sitting down in the chair. "She explained everything to me, and Doc gave her orders that under no circumstances was she to do anything but stay off her feet. Sally, I was wondering if she could stay with you for a while?"

"Yes," she said, "Jake and I have all ready discussed that and I told him it would be okay"

"Thanks," he said, "I appreciate that. Anyway, we need to arrange for her animals to be taken care of and someone to watch her place. So what did you have in mind, Jake?"

"Well," he said, "I think I can get ole Mex to take care of it. He can be trusted and he'll do a good job."

Rich looked at him and said, "I agree."

"Well, then it's done. Now I want to know what you are going to do about all this? I mean, I have kept a careful eye on this girl since her dad died, and it seems to me she's not had any boyfriends that I know of. Now, not that any of this is really any of my business, only that I promised her dad I'd look out after her and I don't recall this being what he asked me to do. I really care about that little gal, so will you clue me in as to what your plans are? I mean, how are you going to take care of her? This whole situation is a real mess, son."

Rich's face turned red and he was speechless for a moment then he said, "Yeah, this is bad, I came along and messed her life up in a big way."

"Never mind that now, what's done is done," said Jake. "It's what you do with this now that counts."

"Do you know she never would have told me if it hadn't come out this way," he said, looking into Jake's eyes. "Said she didn't want to disrupt my life. Disrupt? Hell, Mary's done enough of that to last me a lifetime and I'd like to kill Mary for doing this to her."

"Never mind, Rich," said Jake. "The question now is, does she love you? Bess that is."

"Yes, she does," said Rich.

"And you?" asked Jake. "Do you love her?"

"More than you will ever know," he said. "More than life, Jake. I've lost myself in her and I've loved her so long. It just took me a long time to come to it."

"I kind of figured that, you know. That's why you'd get so mad at me when I'd bring up her name. Well, that's what I wanted to know. Anyway," he said, "how are you going to make it right with her? What kind of plans do you have?"

"Well, I haven't told you or discussed it with anyone except John Bailey, but I started divorce proceedings against Mary right after the storm. I was trying to stop Mary from doing exactly what it was she did. But I guess it wasn't enough, was it?"

Jake thought for a moment. "There's no way she could know about this baby, so I'm thinking you did tell her, didn't you, about the divorce? She does know about the divorce, right?"

"Yes, well, I mean to say, I did tell her and she was hot. Mary doesn't like to give up her property, and she thinks she owns me. She must have suspected we were together and that's why she was there this morning. Jake, I would like to keep this quiet for now to protect Bess."

"Well, don't be surprised if her doctor didn't call the sheriff. What happened is assault and perhaps battery. I don't know the law very well."

"Well, still, I would like to keep this quiet and as much as possible between the four of us for the moment. I want Bethleen protected at all costs."

Jake and Sally had never heard her called this. They just looked at one another, kept their peace and nodded their heads. Sally put her hand on Rich's shoulder, and said, "Don't worry, we'll all get through this."

"You don't know how much all this means to me," he said.

"Yes, we do," she said, "and by the way, I'm going to fix you a sandwich. You must be starved by now."

"Yes, I sure could use something. Thanks, Sally. Jake, do you know where Mex is?"

"Yeah, I think I do."

Sally handed him a plate and he began to eat. "I need to go to her place and get her some things," she said. "It will look better if I'm the one doing it rather than you, only problem being, I don't want to leave her by herself. Do you have any suggestions?"

"Well, I'm sure Mex's wife would run in and do this quietly without anyone knowing what's happening."

Rich's mouth was full and he nodded his head yes in agreement as he put his plate in the sink and said, "I guess we're all set then. I'm going in there and check on her before I leave. I'll catch up with you all later. Sally, thanks for the eats, by the way. I was really hungry."

"You're welcome." She smiled. "Anytime."

He walked in and looked down on her. She was still sleeping soundly, a little tiny bundle she was and she was worried she made trouble for me, when it more like I made a lot of trouble for her. He liked to feel her hair. It was so silky and felt like magic to him. He bent over and kissed her and closed his eyes for a moment. *I'm so sorry, my love,* he thought. *Mary had no right to hurt you, and I'm not going to let her hurt you again. She's going to pay for this, I promise you.* He slipped on his hat and coat and walked out the door.

Chapter Thirty-Two

Bess's dreams were fretful. Her mind went back to the barn and Mary was there, but this time she knew what was going to happen. She tried to hit her back. She moved her body so Mary couldn't touch her, but it went on as before and she hurt. *Ohhhh, I don't feel so good.* She moaned and Mary hit her again. Her face was sore and she was cramping, her body and mind in a deep sleep. *I can't lose my baby. Please, not the baby* she begged and she moaned again.

Chapter Thirty-Three

Sally watched her toss and turn. She had given Bess the medication that her doctor had sent with her. *I should have put her into my spare bedroom*, she thought. *She would be so much more comfortable.* It worried Sally the moaning that Bess was doing. She covered her up and touched Bess's hair, the color of it a red gold brown. *This is a hard situation for everyone. I've always liked this gal, I hope someone somewhere is looking out after her.* Sally sat in her rocker and picked up her knitting bag and began moving the needles without looking at them. Sally was glad she had help at the feed store, it gave her relief when things went awry.

Sally sat there thinking about the first time it had really dawned on her that Rich and Bess had felt something for each other. It was at the Granger girl's wedding, as a matter of fact. And to her recollection Rich had asked her to dance. The way he looked at her and she at him was like any fairytale she had ever seen. Then up blew Mary, big as life, and everyone could see she was hoppin' mad. She strutted up and almost pulled those two apart. *Bess is the lady of the two,* Sally thought. She excused herself and said she had work to do in the kitchen anyway. It was clear to Sally that Rich was none too happy about Mary's little escapade. *But,* she thought to herself, *he never went near Bess again the rest of the evening, not to dance, not to talk, and not even to walk by her. I suppose I can hardly blame Mary altogether, I know I would defend my territory too. But, and there's a big but here, I don't really think she deserves to defend hers. She's always out cattin' about anyway. Some women lose their rights and should when they do that. Why,* she thought to herself indignantly, *you would think Rich would catch her at it sooner or later. It's not like it isn't all over this town.*

Sally wondered how all this was going to turn out. Rich loves her, that's clear, and you can see she nuts about him. *That's not the problem, though,* she thought. *How is Mary going to take all this when she finds out about the baby, and she will, I have no doubt. This is too small of a town for her not to hear.*

She kept the stitches going as fast as her mind was racing, with a watchful eye on Bess. She was moaning and fussing in her sleep and this worried Sally.

I wonder if I should call her doctor? she thought. Sally laid down her hook and tiptoed to her bedroom and dialed his office.

"Hi," she said, "this is Sally Johnson. Is it possible that I could talk to Dr. Bingham? Yes, this is concerning Bess Cramer. Yes, he saw her this morning. Yes, I'll wait."

The house was quiet and she could hear the ticking of her clock. "Hello, Dr. Bingham? This is Sally Johnson and I'm taking care of Bess Cramer. I have a few questions I need to ask you about her if I could. I'm keeping her feet elevated like you asked, and she's sleeping right now, but she's moaning in her sleep and I don't know if she's in pain or what. Yes, and I was wondering if I should wake her or what. Let her sleep for now? Okay. What about food? I don't think she had anything to eat since this morning, if that. No, she hasn't. What can I feed her? Okay, uh-hum, something light, such as soup, jello, sandwich. Would turkey be okay? All right, and if she starts bleeding or cramping bring her to the hospital right away. Yes, I'm writing all this down. Yes, if there's any change, I'll bring her right away. Thanks, Doc."

Sally went immediately to her kitchen cupboards and looked for soup. She found one and opened the can and started the chicken noodle heating. She dug through her refrigerator and found the turkey. She made a light sandwich, poured the soup in a bowl and poured a small glass of milk.

She is pregnant after all, she thought, and Sally smiled to herself. Sally sat the tray on her coffee table and gently touched Bess.

"Bess," she said quietly. "Bess." She shook her carefully. "Bess honey, wake up. You need to eat."

"Huh," she said sleepily, and opened her eyes.

"You need to eat, hon," Sally said. "How do you feel?"

"Not so good, Sally. Where's your bathroom? I feel so weak and I'm cramping."

"I'm going with you, hon. I'll take you there." Sally helped her walk through her living room and dawn the hall.

"I feel real sick," she said, sitting on the pot. "Sally, I don't feel so well at all." Her voice was weak.

"We'll get you back to bed, hon," Sally started to say, when she spotted what was in the pot when Bess got up.

She almost panicked. "Sweetie, I think we had better go see old Doc," she said calmly, "and have him check you out." She ushered her carefully into the living room and sat her on the couch. "Just sit there a minute while I make a short phone call."

Bess nodded her head slowly. Sally made a beeline for the bedroom and dialed Jake's number. "Jake, she's bleeding— find Rich and meet me at the hospital, okay? Okay, bye." Sally got Bess into her coat. *Her eyes—they look glassy, she's not focusing,* she thought. She slid Bess into her old car, shut the door, climbed into the driver's seat and sped off.

Chapter Thirty-Four

Jake felt a sense of panic, and he wished on this day that he hadn't even gotten out of bed. *Or at least he could start it over again,* he thought. He hadn't seen Rich for hours, not since he had sent him to find old Mex. At this moment he wished he knew where he'd gone. Jake had called Bess's place and there wasn't any answer, but then that didn't mean anything. Rich had mentioned a haircut. Now Jake knew the shop was closed, so he called Larry at home anyway. Larry said he had seen him, said he had opened the New Beginnings earlier in the day and he'd given him a cut and a shave.

"Did he say where he was going to?" he asked him.

"No," Larry said, "not a word. Nothing came up in our conversations. In fact, he was unusually quiet."

Jake thanked him and tried the café. Kathy answered, "Yes, I saw him late in the afternoon. He had a quick cup of coffee, and oh, Jake, by the way, Rich was asking me if I'd seen Mary, he was looking for her."

Crap! he thought, he didn't like the sound of that. "Thanks, Kathy," and he hung up. Just for the heck of it, he buzzed the intercom at the barn. No one answered. Jake scratched his head, then he had a thought. *Maybe he went back there hoping to see Bess.* He picked up the phone again and called Sally's. The phone rang and rang and rang. This gave him an uneasy feeling. *Where the heck are you?* he thought.

Jake grabbed the keys to his pickup and he ran out the door. He jumped in and took off down the road. He thought, *Where would I be if I were Rich? Hmmmmm.* He swung past Sally's, but there wasn't any sign of his rig. He went past the grocery store, then he took a quick swing through the downtown area. *Maybe he is at Bess's and no one answered the phone,* Jake thought to himself. *I'll drive out there, and if he's not there I'm heading to the hospital my way.*

Jake's foot pressed harder on the gas. His adrenalin was pumping and his heart was beating fast, he knew he was speeding, but it was his hope that a cop wasn't around. Jake got to the Five Corners cut off, and let up on the gas when he saw the flashing lights on the cop cars about a mile down the road on the Stock Drive cut off. It looked like a nasty accident. "Well, I can't take that cut off, and I'll just have to take Tunnel Hill Road," he said aloud.

When Jake pulled into Bess's, he saw Rich's pickup. *Thank God,* he thought. *Why didn't I come here in the first place? No, I had to do this the hard way. I could have saved myself a lot of trouble if I had.*

Jake was furious with himself for wasting so much valuable time. He jumped out of his pickup and ran to the front door, but no one was in the house. The lights were on so he knew someone was around. Jake looked out the kitchen window. He saw lights on in the barn and his feet flew into a run. He threw open the door and the bright lights hit him. He covered his face and took a quick look around. It told him they had been there, but were gone. Jake just shook his head, then he threw open the door in the back. He saw a flash and he started running again. Down in the field was a truck of some sort and it had its spotlight burning, and on the ground was what looked like Mex and Rich working with one of Bess cows. Jake ran as fast as his legs would carry him, and just as he arrived Rich had pulled the calf, and a heifer was born. The old cow looked around and her eyes got real big and she mooed then. She reached back to kiss and clean her beautiful baby.

"It always amazes me when these animals are born," said Rich to Mex. Then he realized Jake was bent over next to him with both hands on his knees trying desperately to catch his breath. "Jake, what's up? Why you been running? What's the matter?" He said one right after another.

Jake couldn't catch his breath. "Come," he said panting. "Come with me. Hospital, Bess, hurry."

That's all it took. Rich jumped up, he said, "Mex, you're on your own. I've got to go."

The old Mexican crossed his body with the sign of the cross and he said as if he understood what was going on, "I will say a prayer, senor."

Rich just nodded his head and followed Jake at a dead run. Jake pointed to take his truck and they both jumped in, only Rich was driving. It took Jake awhile to catch his breath, but when he did he explained to him everything he knew and at this point it wasn't very much.

Then he told Rich. "We need to take the Tunnel Hill Road, it looked like there was a real bad accident on Stock Drive. I looked all over town for you," Jake said," and several people said you were looking for Mary. I even called Sarah's place, but I didn't get an answer."

Rich left the silence between them for a moment, then he said, "I was looking for Mary, Jake, so I could kill her. I have my 30-30 loaded sitting in my pickup. I planned to do her in and no one was going to stop me. She has more poison, that bitch has, then any human being has a right to, and she has destroyed more lives than anyone I've ever known. I won't let her ever," he said coldly, "and I mean ever, touch Bess again. She's mean. She's the devil herself. If I have my way, she'll be dead before the week is out."

Jake sat there quiet. He had never remembered hearing Rich talk this way before. The quiet demeanor he had was the scariest of all. Jake said very carefully, "You don't think I haven't had my thoughts, and don't you believe that maybe I'm angry too, or that I'm going to stand by and watch her tear into that little gal in two. No, don't you bet on it, Bud. I may beat you to the punch, but at this moment that is the least of our worries. Right now we need to take care of Bess first."

As they pulled into the hospital, there was an ambulance backing up to the emergency doors. And the sheriffs truck still had its lights flashing as it pulled in beside it. "That must have been some wreck," Jake said.

"Yeah, you're right," Rich answered. He looked up at the stars and just shook his head.

They could see Sally pacing through the double doors. She looked frazzled, but her face registered relief when she saw them.

"How's she doin'?" Rich asked.

Sally took his hand and put her arm through it. "She's..." and it caught in her throat, "...she's not doing too good at the moment."

Rich's eyes misted. He shook his head, running his fingers though his hair, his shoulders slumped and he started to pull away. Sally turned him around and faced him. "There's nothing we can do, Rich. What will be will be. They need to stabilize her. She never should have gone home, she should have stayed here. But that's neither here nor there. Rich, she's lost so much weight after you left her. It's more than her little body can take right now. This is what is going against her at the moment, she's just so weak. The doctor says she doesn't have a lot of fight left in her. Rich, there's only one thing we can do for her and that's pray, and pray like you have never prayed in your life before."

Rich walked away, "Can I see her?"

"No, not at the moment. They are still working on her. Come on, Rich, sit here and I'll get you a cup of coffee."

Jake sat quiet on the couch, thinking, "Someone should kill that bitch," he said.

Sally gasped."Jake, that won't solve anything and you know it. Both of you need to remember what goes around comes around."

Jake didn't say anything.

Rich sat there thumbing through magazines and then he set them down. Then he started to rub his legs back and forth. Finally he stood up. When Sally brought back the coffees, Rich said, "Thanks, Sally, but could you hold on to mine for a few?"

"Sure," she said.

"Do you know where the chapel is?"

"Just down through that door and to the right."

"Okay," said Rich and he left.

Sally sat down next to Jake. They sat there for a few minutes, and then Jake said "When do you suppose we'll hear something?"

"I don't know, Jake. Your guess is about as good as mine, and right now mine's not very good."

He nodded his head yes. "When you were back there, you didn't happen to hear who it was they brought in did you?"

"No," she said, "but I think it was a real bad one though. There sure is a lot of commotion going on back there."

"When Rich and I came in, it looked like there was a bad one at the Stock Drive cutoff. There sure were a lot of cop cars there anyway."

Sally brushed a piece of hair from her face. "It feels like a bad night, Jake. I don't know why it does, it just does. My stomach has that ucky feeling I get when something's terrible wrong, and I know it feels like more than just Bess. I have the chills, too."

He reached out and put her hand in his, then he gently put his arm around her and pulled her close to him, only silence and their thoughts between them.

Chapter Thirty-Five

The chapel was quiet and it gave him a sense of peace. Rich knelt down on his knees and folded his hands. "Lord, I know I haven't been on my best behavior, especially tonight. And the harm I've done to others, well, please forgive me. I don't think I've even been a very good husband to Mary or she wouldn't have strayed so far, but for all these things I'm sorry. I'm truly sorry. Now, Lord, I'm asking for that beautiful lady in the other room. Honestly, I didn't mean any harm. I simply fell deeply in love with her. And, Lord, well, She's the kindest, most gentle, woman I've ever known. I don't want her to lose our baby, Lord, but more than that I don't want to lose her. I promise to make it right with her and with you. Please, Lord, please help her to be okay. Take her into your fold and protect her and the baby. No more cussing and no more thoughts of killing people. I'll let you guide me and I'll try harder to be a better man. Amen."

Rich sat there for the longest time with his eyes closed, not moving, listening to his shallow breathing. It was the only sound in the room.

Chapter Thirty-Six

The sheriff hadn't seen such a mangled mess in a long time. They found Mary still alive, but barely, in the grass fifty feet from the wreck. Sarah was pinned and still strapped in her seat belt. They were using the Jaws of Life to get her out. This made it difficult for him, knowing both these women so well. He had to pretend in his mind they were strangers and that he didn't care. Most people didn't know he was crazy about Sarah, their relationship was so far a quiet one, or so he thought. The first ambulance pulled out with Mary, its lights were flashing and the siren was loud. It made him shiver for the first time since he had stood at his first accident scene. Jeff wished they would hurry up, Sarah's color wasn't good.

She kept whispering, "I'm sorry I didn't mean to."

Jeff wanted to reach out and hold her, but his instinct kicked in and he knew she would be better off if he stayed out of the way of the fireman. They were working feverishly to get her loose. *God! what a mangled mess*, he thought.

"Can't you guys go any faster?" he hollered.

Sam came up and put his hand on Jeff's shoulder. "They're going as fast as they can, Jeff," he said sympathetically.

This startled him and he turned and looked into Sam eyes, "You know?"

"Yeah, Jeff, it's been obvious for a long time now, and I'm not the only one who has noticed that you're crazy about her, so, just for protocol's sake, how about we say you head for the hospital. You're not needed here and you might like to get a handle on this."

"Who's babysitting who now?" said Jeff.

"Well, I owe you one. You saved my life. Besides, you need to get a hold of Mary's parents and you don't need to watch this. We'll get her there as quick as we possibly can. There's nothing for you to do here."

"Yeah, I know, it's tearing me apart. I think I'll do just that," he said." I'll head out, but please don't let anything happen to her, okay?"

"Sure, boss, you want me to tell Bob he's in charge?"

"Yeah, but only because we need to stroke him. I don't want to ruffle his feathers," he said with a half grin. Jeff took one last look at Sarah. Her eyes came open, and for a brief moment they met, then she winced in pain and closed them again. This was more than he could deal with, so he turned into the night and quietly slipped away.

Chapter Thirty-Seven

Rich hadn't expected an audience when he walked out of the chapel, but standing in front of him was Sally, Jake, and the sheriff. They all had a grave look on their faces like they had just been to funeral. He looked from one two another and finally said with a frown on his face, "What?"

The sheriff looked at him like, "I'm not sure I want to talk about this," and then he looked away. His hat in hand and eyes to the floor, he shook his head. "Rich, I know you have a lot on your plate right now and I really don't want to add any more to it," then he looked up and their eyes met, "but there isn't a choice, son. We just brought Mary in and it definitely is not good."

Rich was startled, he took in a deep breath.

The sheriff continued, "Her and Sarah have been drinking tonight. We found the bottle and could smell the booze, it's that strong. Anyway, Mary, well, she's in real bad shape. They, the girls, missed the corner, flipped the car. My guess going at a high rate of speed."

Rich listened quietly, shaking his head.

"Mary is in worse shape than Sarah at this moment and, Rich, from the preliminary findings we are pretty sure that Mary was thrown out. Why she wasn't wearing a seat belt when she hit, I don't know. Your guess is as good as mine. They are working on her now in the emergency room. I've been sent to find you, they need you to sign some papers. I'm sorry, Rich. If there's anything I can do."

"Yes," he sighed, his voice froggy, "you call Deanie and Wess."

"Been done already, in fact, they are on their way."

"Thanks," he said. "I appreciate that."

The sheriff started to walk away when he turned around and faced Rich. "I don't want you to take this personal like," he motioned with his hands, "but I'm going to have my say and you can take it or leave it, that's strictly up to you, and then you can deal with it any way you like. I know about your situation with Bess." Rich looked alarmed. "Sally and Jake thought I should know, they meant no harm by it. Now don't go get in a huff," said Jeff. "I already knew, anyway, because her doctor reported to me this morning about the beating she took, and if Mary weren't here right now as we speak, I would be lodging assault charges against her. I also know about your baby, Rich. What you do with your life is your own, and none of my damn business. But I want to give you a bit of advice. You don't want Deanie and Wess to find out what you've done, not just yet anyway. They may be nice folks and all, but that's their little girl lying in there fighting for her life and, Rich, don't kid yourself, they are a powerful people. They have more money than you can shake a stick at. You could never win. For what it's worth, Rich, if you want to protect that little gal in there and her baby, I would stay away, as far away as you can until all this gets sorted out."

Rich thought about everything the sheriff had said and nodded his head.

"I'm sorry. I hated to tell you that," he said, "but I wanted to help you avoid trouble, big trouble."

"Thanks, Jeff," said Rich, "I do appreciate that."

Rich headed down the corridor to find Mary's room. The nursing staff caught up with him and he filled in and signed all the paperwork. He waited what seemed like hours until she was returned from x-ray and surgery. He caught up with her in the intensive care unit and by the time he reached her, she was still under from the surgery. He stood at the foot of her bed and looked down on her. She didn't look threatening anymore, and she wasn't the she-devil he knew. She was somebody's little girl who was in bad physical shape. She, though, not much of one, was still the mother of his kids, and she was lying there all alone fighting for her life with an oxygen mask on her battered face. Her arms were bruised and it looked like one had been broken. Both legs were in casts. One was elevated and hanging from a support off the bed. Rich had never seen her looking so bad. *Dear God in heaven what have we done to one another?* he thought. She was still, as if in a deep sleep, and the IV was dripping into her arm. Rich heard the door flap open and the doctor came in. He motioned for Rich to follow him out.

They stepped out the door and the doctor spoke in a low whisper. "I'll be honest with you. It doesn't look real good at the moment. We are doing all we possibly can for her. She's pretty tore up, then you add the alcohol factor that's in her blood system and it makes fighting for her life a lot harder. Have you called the family?" the doctor asked

"They're on their way," Rich said.

"Good," said the doctor. "I'll know more by the time her folks get here and can give you a complete rundown then. In the meantime, if there's any change, I'll let you know. Why don't you head on down to the cafeteria and get yourself a cup of coffee and a bite to eat. I'll have one of the nurses inform you when her family gets here, okay?"

"Yeah, I think I'm going to take you up on that. It's been a long day." Rich walked down the corridor feeling old, as if he had the weight of the world on his chest. He sat down at the table with his food tray and coffee, and put his head in his hands. *This is going to be a long, long night,* he thought. He closed his eyes, and without realizing it, he drifted, drifted to sleep. The noise of the hospital, the banging and clanging of the dishes didn't reach his ears or move the poor tired soul of Rich Gannon.

Chapter Thirty-Eight

Jeff watched as they walked out of Sarah's door, and he followed the doctor around the corner and stopped him. "How's she doing, Doc?"

"Well, let's say she's doing better than her friend right now. She asked to see you, so if you go in, please don't be in there too awful long. She needs quiet and rest."

"Okay, thanks, doctor," said Jeff. He walked into the room and stood there silently. It had been hours since they had begun working with both the girls. He thought he was alone in the room with Sarah, but the curtain fluttered slightly, and just ever so slightly, and not enough for anyone to notice. Jeff sat down on a chair next to Sarah and held her hand. Sarah's eyes fluttered, and she opened them. Looking around, she focused them on Jeff.

"Hi," he said, a gentle quiet in his voice. He reached for her hand.

"Hi," she said weakly.

"Hi, back again," he said quietly, smiling down on her. "What did you girls do? Decide to do party hardy tonight and it got out of hand?"

"I need to tell you what happened, Jeff." Her breathing was raspy.

"Shhhh…" he said, "it isn't necessary to talk now."

"But I caused the accident, Jeff. I'm to blame. God, I didn't think how it would turn out."

"Hon, just get better and then we can go over it."

"No," she said, "I need to tell you, it's important."

"Haaaaaa," he sighed, "if it makes you feel better, I guess I don't have a choice, but promise me you'll sleep after that."

She nodded her head yes. "Mary and I started drinking late in the afternoon. She was sparring for a fight. Mary had been to see Bess this morning and had beat the living crap out of her. She was sure they had slept together when he was lost in the storm. Then she couldn't stand it, she wanted to rub all that in Rich's face. She told me she pulled up to their ranch. I wasn't with her at the time, but her words were: 'Why the dust was flying and I screeched to stop. Rich come out a running and I laughed in his face. Scared you, didn't I? she said. No, he told her, I just didn't know what was going on.

What do you want? he said. I stepped out of my car and shut the door. Then I walked up to the fence and opened the gate and smiled real big. I told him, How about giving me a piece of you? I said very sweetly. And you know what that bastard did? He grabbed my arm, he didn't hurt me, but he got in my face and he told me, you know what, babe, we're through and he pushed me away. That's when I said, Well, if you're thinking about trading me in for Bess, you can forget it. I just beat the shit out of her awhile ago and the poor babe, I saw her pickup parked at the hospital. She looked in real bad shape too.' She told me she was smirking at him. She thought it was so funny. 'YOU, fucking bitch, I ought to beat the shit out of you, he told me when he pushed me down and walked away.' Mary said, 'Can you believe he said that to me?'

"'I started to get in the car,' she said, 'when he hollered HEY and I looked up, he had his 30-30 leveled at me and I got the Hell out of there. I heard the shot ring out and my back window shattered. Why that stupid ass hole he tried to kill me.'

"I told Mary, there's a lot of people who would like to see you dead, and she just laughed. Well, we drank most of the afternoon, then I quit drinking. Mary wanted to go look up Rich. The more she drank, the worse she got, and she was looking for a knockdown dragout with him, she felt invincible. I tried to talk her into letting me drive, but she wouldn't let me. Mary began to spout about all the people she had done things to and then she turned to me, she said, 'I suppose you want me dead too?'

"I told her no, of course not, what makes you think that? By this time Mary is driving over a hundred miles an hour. I asked her to slow down and she just ignored me.

"'Ah come on now, don't tell me you don't know,' she said.

"I said 'Know what?'"

Jeff felt the sweat pouring off his face and he squirmed in his chair. He knew where this was leading. "Hon, I wanted to talk to you about that."

"Please, Jeff, let me finish this." He nodded his head.

"'Surely you're not THAT stupid are you, Sarah?' Mary said.

"I said I don't know what you're talking about."

"'Didn't Jeffy tell you?' she said to me.

"I said, 'What?'

"By then she was slurring her words badly and her driving was scaring the hell out of me.

"'Why Jeffy and I had a screwing good time, we even have a password picked out for our rendezvous. Let's see,' she snarled at me. 'The lady from Redding.' She was laughing hysterically.

"I screamed, 'THAT'S NOT TRUE!' Then I started to cry that's when she told me, 'Well, sweetie, what would you say if I told you he has a little birthmark on his butt that's shaped like a heart?'"

"Oh God," said Jeff, and he rolled his eyes. "I am sorry she's the one who told you." He stood up and walked to the window. "I should have said something a long time ago and this, well, there's no excuse, but she had threatened me and I really didn't want you to know about any of this. Sarah, I don't know how to make this right for you."

"Jeff," she said, "come here and sit. There's more to tell." She squeezed his hand. "It gets worse, much worse, more than I can live with," she said quietly. "I was so angry with her. I put my foot on the gas pedal over hers and just before we crashed I unbuckled her seat belt. I wanted her to die. Oh God, I want her to die," she said sobbing. "It wasn't just my anger; it was all the people she has intimidated and hated over the years. The ones she's deliberately set out to hurt, the friends who befriended her and she betrayed, the parents she hates. I suddenly couldn't stand by and let her poison or hurt anyone, anymore. I'll probably go to jail for this, Jeff, but I'm not made of the same material as her. I felt so bad for what she did to Bess. That gal didn't deserve to be beaten. And you know what? Mary said she didn't even try to fight her back. In Mary's words, she lay there like a whimpering coward. Well, in my book Mary is the coward."

Jeff didn't know what he was going to do with this information at the moment, he just sat there feeling sick inside. "In a way I wish you hadn't confessed all this to me. It leaves me in a strange position. But for now keep this to yourself. I want you to sleep, I've been in here far to long and the nurses will be shooing me out soon."

"Will you stay with me until I fall asleep?"

"Yes, if you say you will forgive me for my indiscretion. You know, Sarah, it only happened one time."

"You've already been forgiven, Jeff, I'm glad you're here."

"I'm glad too, now go to sleep." She closed her eyes and soon she was out like a light. Jeff quietly slipped out the door, and when he was gone the shadow opened the door slightly, looking both ways to see if it was clear, then walked down the corridor.

Chapter Thirty-Nine

Rich had awakened with a start. Someone's hand was on his shoulder. "What…what?" he said as his eyes focused.

It was Mary Margaret the night nurse. "The doctor would like to see you."

Rich looked up and realized he had fallen asleep at the table in the lunchroom. He wondered how long his eyes had been closed. "Sure," he said, "where is he?"

Mary Margaret smiled. "He's in the waiting room talking to your in-laws."

"Thanks, Mary," he said, and off he went.

The corridors in hospitals always seem eerie and cold at night, he thought, *and they sure don't smell very good either.* He went through the swinging doors, and sitting on the couch was the doctor and his in-laws. "I," he said, "I'm sorry. I went to go get something to eat and a cup of coffee and I fell asleep at the table."

"That's alright," said Wess. "Ya look reel drug out. Actually, ya look like hell."

"So do you," bantered Rich with a small grin.

Dr. Ferguson waited until Rich sat down and he continued with Mary's case. "She has a lot of alcohol in her system and this is a contributing factor that is not helping her situation at all. Two broken legs, hairline fracture of the pelvis, one arm is shattered and she's in a coma. If she makes it out of this, she will be real lucky. You asked me to tell it to you straight. Well, it is my opinion if you have a pastor or a priest you should call them, not just for Mary, but also for you."

Deanie did not say anything and was unusually quiet. Wess took her hand and asked her if she was okay? She just sat there, the shock of all this was more than she was able to deal with. "Darlin', are ya okay?" he asked again.

She nodded her head yes and the doctor stood up, he said, "I'm going to order a shot for her." He nodded his head at Deanie. Wess and Rich both shook their heads yes.

"When can I go back in and see her?" Rich asked.

"Well, we are still doing tests on her, Rich, but when we get finished I'll have one of the nurses come let you know. Okay?"

He nodded his head. "Wess, could you excuse me for a few moments? I'll be right back."

"Sure" he said, nodding his head.

Rich dug into his pocket and pulled out several quarters and headed to the phone booth in the hall. He dialed the minister of the First Baptist Church. "John? This is Rich Gannon, I'm sorry to bother you so late, but…" Then he went on to explain to him everything that had taken place that night. "So if you wouldn't mind, I sure would appreciate it if you could come down here tonight. Thanks. I'll tell Mary's folks you are on your way." He hung up the phone and looked in the direction of Wess and Deanie, then he slipped quietly down the hall toward Sally and Jake. They were sitting at the end of the hall by the emergency room. Sally got up and started toward him.

"We thought it would be better for you if we stayed here so as not to alarm them, the Harlows, I mean."

"That's probably a good idea, though I don't think at this moment they would notice anything except what's happening to Mary," he said. Then, changing the subject, "How is she doing? How is Bess?" he said softly

Sally looked at Jake and they both looked at Rich.

Sally spoke, "I wasn't going to tell you, but only because you have so much going on, but we talked it over and decided that even now, with everything else happening, we need to be honest with you."

Rich swallowed hard, he didn't like the sound of this. "Has something happened to her—is she going to be okay?"

"She will be okay in time, Rich, but…"

"But what," said Rich.

"They got the bleeding stopped, Rich, but she…she lost the baby. I'm, I'm so very sorry."

His head went down and a gasping cry came from his throat. "Will she be okay?" he said softly.

"They don't know at this point if she will ever be able to have children, and no, Rich, before you ask, she doesn't know yet. The doctor has decided she's so weak that now is not the time to tell her about it."

"What caused it?" he asked.

"I was hoping you wouldn't ask that, but since you did…"

Jake stood up as if in anticipation of Rich's next move. "It was the severe blow she took when Mary hit her, and then complicated by the fact that she lay on the ground for so long. This baby just didn't have a chance."

Rich rammed his fist into the wall. "I swear by all that's mighty, Mary will pay for this somehow, some way," he said, forgetting the promise.

Jake did the one fatherly thing he could think to do, he put his hand on Rich's shoulder. The two men stood silent for the longest time. "Jake, I could kill her," he said as he turned to him. "I know I promised God to do better, but I could kill her."

Jake looked him in the eyes. "Don't even go there, it's not worth it."

"What about you?" he said. "All I said was I thought I had a way to fix things, Rich. I was talking about money. I have enough to buy her out, that's all. Now listen to me. This is what I need for you to do. First clean up that hand so your in-laws don't wonder why it's bloody, then you're going to leave Bess in our hands. You are going to take care of Mary like a husband would do, should do. We will sort all this out later. I promise you something will be done about Mary, but another day, so for now I want you to just concentrate on what's in front of you."

Rich shook his head, then asked, "Sally, you don't have any aspirin, do you? I have one heck of a headache."

She dug into her purse and handed him a couple and asked, "Is that enough?"

"Yes, thanks," he said. "I'll see you later," and he headed in the direction of the water faucet.

Chapter Forty

It was late very late, almost two a.m. The hospital had finally settled down and all that could be heard was the whispering and low murmurs of the nursing staff. Mary was stable for the moment. At midnight, Wess took his wife home under protest, but he held his ground, and convinced her that she wasn't doing Mary any good sleeping in the waiting room. Besides, he reasoned, the shot the doctor gave her would put her into a deep sleep anyway. So why not be home safe in her own bed where it was quiet. She decided not to put up a fight. Her eyes were so heavy that it was all she could do to get up and navigate to the door.

Rich was going to stay and keep an eye on Mary and unknown to them, Bess too.

"Ya'll call us if thayr's any change?" asked Wess.

"Yes, I will," he said gently. "You go ahead and get her into bed. There's really nothing you can do here anyway."

With everyone gone, Rich sat down in the chair and propped his feet up in another and soon he was out. Mary Margaret came along and thought he needed a cover and so she slipped quietly away and opened the supply closet door and pulled one out. She carefully covered him up so as not to disturb him. Sally had long since sent Jake home, explaining to him that it wasn't needed that they both be here.

"I'll stay and keep an eye on Bess. You have chores to do in the early morning and then more chores to do. So get out of here and let me take care of this end." Well, when Sally made up her mind, she was set and there wasn't any arguing with her. So Jake took his hat, put it on his head, kissed her goodbye, making her promise to call if there were any changes. She went back to Bess' room and sat with her, between dozing and knitting. This was to be her night.

Because of the hour, when all was quiet on the first floor of the hospital, and people were either gone or asleep or in their own domains, the shadow had been watching and waiting very patiently for all of them to settle in. *There is plenty of time,* was the thought, and looking around not to be seen by anyone, the shadow carefully opened up Mary's door. Looking at her chart, it would be awhile before the next nurse would come in. The shadow reached over and took her hand and held it…a low whisper came from the voice, "You're a bad seed." The shadow rubbed the hand in loving affection. This was going to be very difficult, for the shadow had mixed emotions.

The shadow picked up the oxygen mask and took it off of the battered girl's face…her breathing became ragged as the needle pushed the serum in, then it became raspy and she gasped for air until at last she gurgled and blood foamed at her mouth. When the shadow decided she was gone, the mask was replaced on her mouth. A hand reached out and touched her gently, then put the needle in the disposal box. Looking down both corridors making sure all was clear, the shadow paused, looking one last time and quietly walked out the door and disappeared into the night.

Chapter Forty-One

Wess was as a southern gentleman and genteel as Rhet in *Gone With the Wind*. He was shorter then Deanie, but it was clear he adored her. He always wore his silk shirts under his vest and his pants were of the finest, tailored to fit him in his pristine lifestyle. He wore his hair always parted and flat to his head. He had a long nose, but it didn't seem to be noticeable, for under it was his handlebar mustache, groomed to fit his style. In the last few weeks he had weaned himself from the bottle and stood there more sober than he had in many years. He looked at Clydean, saw the pain she was feeling and to him this was more than he could bear...

"You know, Wesley, I can't hardly deal with this," she said softly to him.

He took her gently into his arms and held her for the longest time. "Ah know. darlin'," he said in his southern drawl. "Time will heal all thee's foe ya'll, Clydean."

She pulled back from him and said, "Are you alright? You don't usually call me Clydean, Wesley."

"An ya don't usely call me Wesley ethar," he said, "but ya know yare such a beautiful woman, it is befittin of ya ta have such a stately name, dawlin. I neva told ya much how ah have loved ya all theses yeeas or how much it has meant foe me ta be in yora presence."

"Wesley, what's the matter with you today," she said. She felt panic in her soul. "What's wrong? You tell me now," she said as she looked into his eyes.

"Nothing, dawlin', nothing ole Wesley kan't fix. Now ya'll run along and tell thooz youngins all about theya moma. Yo sho them a real good time...they'll injoy seein they'a momas room when she was jus a pup."

"Wesley," she said quietly, "why have you quit drinking? I've noticed the last few weeks you have slowly stopped and now not a drop."

"Mayba it's time ole Wesley gru up and, basides, som thangs have ta be done soba, dawlin. Now yo run along, sho those babes a good time. I love ya, dawlin', jus ya rememba that I love ya."

"I love you, too, Wesley." Deanie felt uneasy about walking away. It felt final, yet he said everything would be alright, and he never lied to her. She went up the long staircase and took another look at him. He was smiling and waved her on. She saw Amanda her maid making her way to her and she had the kids just shining.

"Thanks, Amanda, you always do such a nice job."

Amanda liked Deanie. She always treated the servants like they were family. The pay was real good and her and Wess never forgot to say thanks and please.

"Thank you, ma'am."

"Now, kids, your grandfather wanted me to take you way across to the other side of this big old mansion on an adventure to show you where your mom spent her younger years. He thought it might be fun for you to see what your mama was like as a little girl. Your Daddy will be here later today to see you. He has some things to do before he comes."

Tylor's head was hanging, "We didn't see much of Mama, but I miss her anyway, Grandmamma. Why did she have to die?"

"I know you do, hon. I miss her too, and I don't know the answer to that question myself." And she hung her arms around this beautiful eight-year-old boy and hugged him. Kayleen was only four years old, but her little hands reached to be lifted up in Deanie's arms. She held her and thought, *How sad, my beautiful daughter will never see these children grown.* Her eyes let a tear drop, then she wiped it away. It wasn't often she let anyone see this side of her, but the children were a different matter all together.

"Amanda," she said, "do you have anything real important due right now?"

"No, ma'am."

"Would you help me, would you come with us to the east end and be there with the children? Please..."

"I would enjoy that, ma'am," she said.

"Thank you," said Deanie.

Wesley looked at old Douglas after Deanie left him, and he asked "How long ya'll ben with me, sah."

Douglas was a proud black man who stood six feet in his stocking feet. He was as gentle and kind as any man Wesley had ever known. "Going on thirty years, sir."

"Have ah always treated you ryet.?"

"Yes, sir."

"Now you woodn't go telling me that to sooth ma soul, would yeah?"

"No, sir. You and the misses have been real good to me, and everyone else that lives on this place. Sir?" He spoke a little louder. "If I may be so bold?"

And the gentleman said, "Proceed, sir" and he gestured with his hand.

"You both treat everyone as if we are family. I don't know of anyplace I could work that would pay for medical insurance, time off when we need it, and even when we don't. The pay is better than any place I've ever seen. And, sir, you don't treat any of us like we are your slaves, black or white. We all have the right to go if we want. When one of us is sick, you tend to our needs like we are your children. No, sir, I like it just fine."

"Ya neva thought ya shood have gone and got an edyukashon? It neva ocurd to ya?"

"No, sir, I'm satisfied. I like it just real fine right here," he said.

"Wool, thank ya vera much foe the infoemayshun," said Wess. "Ah'll make shuwa ya'll arh takein kayeah of. Now ah have sum papers ah have to wook on and ah don't want ta be desturbed. Stand gard foe me an don't let any one in."

"Yes, sir," he said as he stood erect like a soldier.

And with that Wess went in and shut and locked his door. He sat down at his huge old oak desk and opened the drawer. He pulled out three sheets of the fancy paper that had his and Deanie's family emblem on the top. The first letter he addressed to Deanie, the second draft he addressed to Sheriff Baldwin, and the third he addressed to Bess. When he finished, he sealed each envelope, put a name on each and burned wax on the back, then stamped it with their seal, carefully tucking them into his safe. Sitting there for a while, he gazed out his window as if to breathe in all his life's work. He then reached into his drawer and pulled out his old pistol, loaded it and said, "Godd foegive me foe what ah have done an foe what ah am about to do,"…and he pulled the trigger.

Chapter Forty-Two

Douglas was standing guard at the door. He reflected on his conversation with the Mister. He liked him and he was sad that his little girl was gone. Douglas had known grief when he lost his misses and the Mister had been kind. He had given him time off without question and paid for the funeral expenses. He had bought all the flowers and had all the food made for after the service. Douglas had tried to protest, but the Mister would not hear of it and insisted. It was a hard time for Douglas, for his precious misses was all he had in the world. Finally, when he was ready to come back, he was welcomed with love and understanding. This only enhanced his loyalty to the Mister and his wife. *The Mister has been in there a long time,* he thought. *I wonder what he's doing?* Not that Douglas would ever ask. *But the whole conversation had been an odd one,* he thought.

The mansion was a busy place with the normal workings of the day. Some things were different as they prepared for Mary's funeral. The cook was in the kitchen. She had asked for extra help and the lady of the house had said, "Talk to Douglas. He's in charge." This made him feel good to know she counted on him. So he had rounded up the extra help by pulling some of the women from the cookhouse to give Modie a hand in the kitchen. This satisfied her and all the complaints seemed to stop.

This is a big place, he thought, *and it takes a lot of us to run it.* He could see through the glass doors that Ginger was retrieving flowers from the side garden. These he supposed were the ones to be set aside for the funeral. The Mister's wife had given those orders, so he wasn't sure that's where they would go. It was a guess for him. He stood there and let time drift him away, with thoughts of the past and listened to the scurrying all around him.

When he heard the shot ring out, he didn't move. It wasn't the normal sound of the house, so it didn't at first register in his mind. Then a sense of panic set in and he turned and realized it had come from the Mister's door. Douglas hollered loudly, "Are you all right, sir!"

There was silence. Douglas shook off the sick feeling he had in the pit of his stomach. He tried the door, it was locked. Again he shouted, "Are you all right, sir?" and again there was no answer. Douglas was a big man and strong. He stepped back, crossing his arms to give him more push and he ran at the door, busting the lock and breaking into the room. He stood there staring in disbelief. It felt like hours as he stared at what was before him. When a hand came out of nowhere and touched his shoulder. Douglas gasped. He was startled and he swung around defensibly.

"There's nothing we can do for him now," said Rich. Douglas just nodded his head. "Let's get out of here. Douglas, we need to call 911. Don't touch anything, okay?" Rich could see that Douglas was in shock; he was as white as a sheet. "We're going to close these doors," he said as he pulled them shut. "I want you to stand right here." Douglas looked up, his face had a frightened look on it. Rich grabbed him by both arms and looked him in the eye. "I need for you to be strong, Douglas. We can't let anyone in here, especially Deanie."

"Yes sir, I understand," he said.

The old Douglas was coming back and Rich could see he was in charge again. "I'm going to go call the sheriff and I'll be right back. No one, Douglas, but no one can enter those doors except the sheriff, got it?"

"Yes, sir. I'll guard it with my life."

Rich felt so sick to his stomach that he found the bathroom down the hall and puked into the toilet. Not once, but twice. He hurriedly wiped his mouth and ran out into the hall and picked up the phone. He dialed. *Troubles, troubles, troubles,* he thought. *First Bess, then Mary, now Wess. What else will the day bring?* as he waited for the phone to stop ringing.

Chapter Forty-Three

It had been a long week for Jeff with the death of Mary, and he was still wrestling with the information Sarah had given him. He thought about all the pros and cons of the situation. It occurred to him that if he discussed his conversation with anyone that Wess and Deanie could and would see to it that Sarah would spend the rest of her natural life in jail, or at the worst it could mean murder one. *If I keep this to myself,* he thought, *could I really live with it? Can I do this to someone I love? Then again, I'm honor bound to keep the laws. I'm so tired,* he thought. *I'm tired of all this and I'm getting too old. Maybe I should give up being a cowboy cop. Who needs all this power anyway. I don't really have to do this job, do I?* he thought. *I have plenty of dough, Ah shit, what the hell am I going to tell Sarah? I sure have made a mess of things.* Jeff had been sitting at his desk for a long time running through all the pictures and thoughts in his mind. When he heard the door open and looked up, it was Sam peeking through the door.

"Are you all right, Jeff?"

"Yeah, I'm fine," he said.

"You don't look so fine, in fact, you look like death warmed over," said Sam.

"It's been a long rough night," he said. "But come on in, Sam, and set a spell. Tell me one of your funny stories to cheer me up."

Sam had pulled up a chair and sat down when the door blew open again. This time it was Deputy Lupe and she stepped through the door.

"Sheriff, you have been in here a long time and, well, I'm not a waitress or any thing but would you like a cup of coffee? And before you say anything like 'oh boy what a miracle,' let me say this. I am worried about you, sir. You don't look so good."

He laughed. "I promise I won't say a word, but would you mind getting Sam one too? That is if I make him promise not to say, 'oh boy what a miracle?'"

She laughed. "Only if he promises me a date later tonight when I get off work." Sam hadn't expected this. He turned with his eyebrow raised and looked at her.

"I'm expecting an answer from you when I return and with the coffee." She smiled and shut the door behind her.

Jeff looked at Sam and grinned a big grin. "Whew," he said, "I guess you know she's got the hots for you ole buddy. And in case you haven't noticed, it's been going on for some time."

"No, I haven't. I'll be honest, Jeff, I had no idea. I guess I've had my head in the sand."

"Well, what you've had is a bad case of mistaken love, and with that, I mean Bess Cramer, of course, and I'd say that's a lost cause now."

Sam shook his head in agreement. Just then the deputy came through the door with two cups of coffee. She handed the sheriff his and then she reached over to give Sam his coffee, but her hand lingered on the cup. "Well," she said, "what's the answer?"

Sam sized her up and down. He thought to himself, *She's not bad at all, you know, and I'd say I've been missing out.* "Just let me know when," he said.

"How about tonight when I get off at eleven?" she said.

"There won't be anything open at that hour, you know?" he said.

"I know," she said, smiling. "That's the whole point. Dinner at my house, Sam, and then who knows what. See you then?"

"Yeah, sure," he said, a bit baffled. And she closed the door behind her.

Jeff laughed. "WOW!" touching his hand like it was sizzling hot, "She is smokinnn'. There for a moment I thought I was going to have to leave the room."

"Ah, cut it out, Jeff," he said, and Sam's face got red.

"Now drink your coffee, bud, and tell me that funny story."

"Well, I don't know how funny this is, but it's a story about my brother and me. When I was just a kid…"

Jeff interrupted, laughing, "Hell, Sam, you're still just a kid," he said.

"No, I mean when I was just a little pisser." With this, it made Jeff laugh even more. "Ah, come on, Jeff. Let me tell the story," he said.

"Okay. I'll shut up." He grinned.

"Anyway, we lived way up in the mountains. You see, now my step-dad was a sheep herder. Well, anyway, it was way too far to come down to school, so our mom boarded us out at Mrs. Mahoney's house. She had a boy who was about our age and his name was Roy. So, when Roy, my brother Tom and I got together what one couldn't think up the other would. We were always up to no good; we were plain just mischievous boys. One day we heard the two women talking, my Mom and Mrs. Mahoney, about the bachelor up the road, and that he had a live-in housekeeper. Well now, in those days it was unheard of for a single woman and a single man living under the same roof together. Not without imagining some sort of hanky panky goin' on. The ladies quite often talked about this woman, but they called her old lady whistle britches, not by her given name. That was their code name for her when she would walk by, or they would see her coming. Just being boys, we caught onto this conversation and we knew it was gold. We couldn't wait to try this out. So one day after school we deliberately cut across a field so we would walk right by her place and she just happened to be outside. So, in unison we hollered, 'Hello, Mrs. Whistle Britches.' Well, I'll have you know she promptly made her way to Mrs. Mahoney's house and demanded to know where the boys came up with this title. Of course, both women denied having any knowledge of the whereabouts of this new name we called her. When she left we knew we were in deep shit. Now, my mom was a big woman and Mrs. Mahoney wasn't small by no means. A woopin' by either one would be a severe blow, not only to our egos but to our butts as well. They gathered us up and gave us a choice. We either go apologize, or we get the lickin' of our lives. Well, we trekked down to her place and I'll have you know we were not looking forward to this. She was sitting in a chair in her kitchen right in the middle of the floor. I went in first and told Mrs. Bain I was sorry, then Roy, and when he was done, my brother Tom stood outside kickin' the dirt under his shoes and said, "There ain't no way I'm going in there to apologize to that woman." I was sure in my mind there was no way he was ever going to go do it either, that he had made up his mind. I smiled and Roy looked at me. He nodded his head and I mine, we knew exactly what we were going to do. I grabbed one side of my brother and Roy the other and we threw him in the house. Well, you know he skidded about fifteen feet on his knees. He ended up sliding with his hands clasped in prayer, and instead of calling her by her formal name, Mrs. Bain, he spoke rapidly. 'I'm sorry I called you old lady whistle britches,' he says. By now Roy and I are rolling on the ground we were laughing so hard. The lady reached out and boxed his ears and about that time he said, 'Sorry, Mrs. Bain, I won't do it again.'"

Jeff was in stitches he was laughing so hard. "I bet you never called her that again, did you?"

"No," said Sam laughing. "And don't say it, I know already know it. I was an ornery little fart. Besides, by then my brother could have killed us both."

"I'll bet," said Jeff.

The phone rang and he picked it up, "This is Jeff." His face turned grave. "How long ago? Did you touch anything? Okay, well don't. No one is to go in there and don't touch anything. Yeah, Rich, I'm on my way right now. No, someone from here will call them. Okay, bye."

Sam looked at him puzzled. "So what's up, bud?"

Jeff just shook his head. "It looks like ole Wesley blew himself away. My guess is he couldn't do without his daughter Mary."

"No shit," said Sam. "What next?"

"I don't know," said Jeff, and he grabbed his keys, "We better go, and this time I want you with me," and they walked out and shut the door.

Chapter Forty-Four

Sometimes life just keeps on hitting hard, never easing up or backing away. This was one of those times and Rich felt the cards he had been dealt were not in his favor. He was tired, so very tired and this was too much to deal with. He knew that Deanie would fall apart. That Wess and her had been partners, not just lovers and friends. *How am I going to break this news to her?* he thought. He felt sick, and, *What about the kids?* he thought. *They are just now dealing with their mother's death, how are they going to understand losing their grandfather? Do I tell them the truth? The kids are so young maybe it's better I don't go into details. After all, he was so much a part of their lives and he loved them. So why would he do this? Losing Mary is not the end of the world. There are so many people he left behind that love him. This just doesn't seem to make any sense to me and I know it won't to Deanie. I need to be here for her and the kids.* Rich's mind was racing and it felt as if his head would explode. He had managed to block out the noise around him for the last hour. Now suddenly they filled his mind like a locomotive crossing the tracks right in front of him.

He listened as the attendants lifted the gurney and slipped out the door, his eyes following the body bag that lay on top of it. One of the attendants looked over at him, her eyes filled with sadness and compassion.

"Hurry up, Charlie," she said as she pushed the gurney faster. Charlie didn't say anything, he just lifted it gently out the door and down the steps. Rich put his head down and he began to cry. *Grown men don't cry,* he thought, *but I can't seem to stop,* and the tears flooded his being. He stood so no one could see him and leaned onto the fireplace.

"Rich," said Jeff quietly, as he stood facing him, "this is what we have at this moment, and you understand it's only the preliminary findings. We believe the shot was self-inflicted. But, of course, we have to wait for the autopsy results and to see if he has powder burns on his hand. The crime scene investigators will have to come to some conclusion one way or the other.

Anyway, at this point it looks like it was self-inflicted and no one else was involved. We sent Deputy Lupe down to talk to Deanie and let her know what happened. My guess, Rich, is that second ambulance was for her."

"Oh my God I don't know what I was thinking, I forgot the kids were with her," said Rich, panicking. "My kids are there, Jeff, with her, I have to go." His voice was pleading as he headed out the door.

Jeff caught him carefully by the arm, and said, "When you get things settled with them come back and see me, will you? I have a few questions for you that I need answered. Just routine you know. Okay?"

"Yeah, sure, now please, can I go?" Rich said, searching Jeff's eyes.

"Yeah, go ahead," he said and he let go of his arm.

Chapter Forty-Five

The sheriff sat back at his desk rehashing this last weeks events. He looked out the tiny window in his office and could see what was left of the sunset. Jeff picked up the phone and dialed the hospital.

"Karon, this is Sheriff Baldwin, could you give me the status on Clydean Harlow? Sure, I'll wait," he said, tapping his fingers. He wondered how Sarah was. *My beautiful Sarah,* he thought. "Yes," he said aloud. "I'm glad she's sleeping. No, I don't want to disturb her, not after what she's been through. She can use all the rest she can get. She's a strong woman doctor, but…" he was concerned and shaking his head, "…but I really think someone should be near by just to keep an eye on her. You have! Oh good, I'm real glad to hear that. I'll check back with you in the morning and see how it's going. Could you have someone patch me through to room 213? Thanks, Doc."

Jeff tapped his pencil on the desk while he waited, and listened to the music provided for his listening pleasure. He laughed out loud. *Do they really think any of us enjoy this crap?* Then the phone began to ring and a sleepy Sarah said a quiet hello.

"Hi, Sarah, I know it's late and I wanted to let you sleep, honey, but I want to check in with you before you closed your eyes and went off to dreamland."

"Hi, Jeff," she said quietly. "You sound tired."

"I am," he said. "Real tired, but I didn't call to talk about me. I called to see how you are doing."

"I'm fine. In fact, if everything goes well, tonight I'll be out."

"Then I'll call you later and see if they are going to release you and come and get you. I'll be your taxi cab."

"I'd like that," she said. "Jeff? I heard whispering in the hall that Wess shot himself. Is it true?"

"Yeah, he did. But I don't want you to bother yourself about that now I just want you to get well."

He could hear her softly crying in the background. "Sarah, don't blame yourself. You didn't kill Mary and you're not to blame. Someone else took that out of your hands when she was there. Don't think about this right now, please. I just want you well enough to get out of here. Okay?"

"All right," she said blowing her nose. "I'm a little tired now, so I'm going to rest for awhile."

"You do that, sweet Sarah, you do that," and he hung up the phone. *Why, he thought to himself, why didn't I tell her how much I care for her? Because it's not the right time,* he thought. *Nope, not the right time,* as he shook his head back and forth.

Chapter Forty-Six

Crane didn't like the fact that he and his partner were going to have to question the sheriff. However, in their investigation Jeff's name came up as one of Mary's conquests. He knew that it was important to touch all bases and it would be better to clear the sheriff of all wrongdoing now, then they could let it go. Smith had gone to Jeff's office to politely ask him to stop in; they had a few things they wanted to ask him. Simply a casual conversation, nothing official, of course. Just a courtesy call. Crane did not like this at all. This could affect promotions or cause hard feelings. He really didn't want to stir the pot, so to speak. When the door opened, Crane was explaining to Jeff that it was better to talk in here, what with the privacy and all. "Besides," he said, "this way you will get away from the phones for a few minutes."

"Yeah, right," said Jeff. "You just want to get me in here to intimidate me."

"No," said Crane, "I have to do this. I don't have any choice. We have a lot of people on our list. I was surprised to see your name crop up. Go ahead, Jeff, sit here," he said. And he pulled out the chair facing the mirror.

"Okay, I'll play your game," he said, and he sat down.

As the two detectives pulled out their chairs, they squeaked across the floor, causing an echoing sound in the almost empty room. They looked at one another as if the silent signals would not be read by anyone else in the room.

Jeff thought to himself, *They really think I am that stupid*, and he silently shook his head.

"Would you like some coffee?" Crane asked politely

"No," he shook his head, "no thanks. I'm coffeed out."

"You know you're not under arrest Jeff, but we could read you your Miranda and or provide you with a lawyer. If you like, we can get a union rep in here for you, too."

"No," said Jeff, "let's just get this over with."

"Are you sure you don't want your union rep?"

"NO! Let's just get this done so I can get back to work. I've got lots to do."

Jim Smith nodded his head to Bill Crane and gave him the go ahead. "Can you tell us what you were doing on October fifth this last year?"

"How the hell should I know what I was doing back then?" he said, raising his voice. "Who can remember that far back?"

Crane and Smith both made a personal note that Jeff was avoiding their eyes. "We have a witness, a person who said they saw you with Mary going into the Inn's Motel on October fifth. Got anything to say about that?"

Jeff sat there. He wasn't sure what his next move would be. His best bet he knew was just tell it like it was. "Who told you that?" he asked.

"Now you know we can't reveal that to you."

Jeff sat there quiet for a moment, finally he said, "Yes I was with her but only that one time, and I'm sure I'm not the only dick in town she's fooled with."

"No probably not," said Crane, "but we also know you have been dating Sarah and we figured you don't want her to find out about it." He leaned across the table and looked into Jeff's eyes. "We also know that Mary has called you here at the station a couple of times and one of them you were screaming your head off. So I'd say you have good reason to not want her to live. We think like maybe she was blackmailing you."

"Good reasons maybe, yes, but I didn't and I wouldn't," said Jeff. "Besides, Sarah already knows all about it. So Mary couldn't have blackmailed me."

"And what did Sarah have to say?" said Smith as he took more notes.

"None of your God damn business, Smith. If you want to know, ask her."

"Oh, I plan to do just that," he said, and he rose to grab Jeff's shirt. Bill Crane stopped him short and pushed him into the wall.

"Cool off, Jim," he said. "We don't want any trouble, just the facts, buddy. Just the facts."

"Yeah, okay, sure, sure thing," he said, pulling his shirt back down. He pulled out his chair giving the sheriff a dirty look and sat down.

"You were freely walking around the hospital the whole night Mary died, and given your feelings about her, you could have easily done her in and no one would be smart enough to put two and two together and no one would suspect you. Why they wouldn't even look your way."

"I didn't, Bill, and you know it. Screwing a woman for a one-night stand does not constitute a good enough reason to kill her. Besides, I was surrounded by people I knew. You can ask Karon and Mary Margaret. They saw me, and what about all the doctors on call?"

"You could easily slip away from them all, you know," said Jim. "There were a lot of people milling around and you could of slipped in and out without anyone noticing."

"Yeah, but I didn't. What WAS the exact hour of her death anyway? And what's the coroner have to say, have you talked to him yet? And by the way, has the toxicology report come in yet?"

"Whoa, slow down there, bud. One question at a time. She died at 2:00 a.m., Jeff, from what Krandell told us, and as far as the toxicology report, it is not in as yet, but listen tell me. I want to know where you were at that hour of the morning, Jeff? Do you have an alibi, someone who can verify your whereabouts?"

"As a matter of fact I do." He grinned. "Sam and I were just finishing up our dinner at the All Night Diner. Because of the accident and Bess Cramer's beating, you do remember she was hospitalized that night, don't you? Anyway, with everything that happened that night we hadn't eaten so we took chow together."

"You know, of course, we will have to verify this, check it out with Sam and with the diner?"

"Yeah, I understand, so can I go now? I have paperwork to do and I want to go by the hospital and see Sarah."

"Sure, but I caution you, we need to ask you not to discuss this case with anyone, and that includes Sam, Sarah, or anyone else for that matter, until we can verify all your facts."

"That's an understatement, don't you think? I don't have any intention of discussing anything with anyone."

When the door slammed behind Jeff, Bill and Jim looked at each other. "His alibi will more than likely check out you know, mainly because his butt is on the line, but also he knows we can check this out real easy," said Bill.

"Yeah, well, I wish it wouldn't, I'd like to have a piece of that man," said Jim.

"Come on, forget it. Let's go to the diner and see what we can dig up. Besides, I'm getting hungry and a cup of coffee right about now sounds real good to me." Bill gently tugged on his partner of twelve years and finally Jim gathered up his overweight body out of his chair and started for the door.

He stopped before he opened the door and looked Bill in the eyes. "It would give me great pleasure to handcuff that man. I don't think I have ever disliked a man as intensely as him."

Bill looked at him. "You think it would be worth all your trouble, all that just because he ran against you in the race and won? Come on, Jim. Do you think you would really like to be in his shoes right now?"

"I don't know, but I sure would like to try," he said as he opened the door and they both walked out.

Chapter Forty-Seven

Charlie Sargent had been watching all three with interest. In fact, he had sat in at the mirror and had heard the whole conversation. He wondered what they were whispering about when they came out the door. He wasn't too particularly fond of Jim Smith, and had been real glad he hadn't won the last race. He was nearing his pension and really didn't want to spend the last of it with Smith in charge. Smith had a bad temper and this related to everything he did. He was unpleasant and those around him did not like him. The only one who seemed to get anywhere with him was his partner of twelve years, and sometimes even he had trouble keeping him in line. Someone like that didn't belong in charge of a whole crew; it would only serve to cause trouble internally, and that wouldn't do. Charlie had been at it long enough to know it took teamwork with everyone to pull the cases together. Sugar always worked better than sour grapes, he'd say. Charlie had been quietly investigating this case on his own. He only had a few weeks left, and then it wouldn't matter if he tangled with Smith anyway. *I mean, what's he going to do to me?* he thought. *Shoot me?* and he laughed out loud. Everyone in the room looked at him and the sounds echoed in the room.

"What's so funny, Charlie?" someone asked.

"Yeah, what's so funny?" someone else said.

"Private joke," he said. "Nothing I want to share with any of you, thank you." Then Charlie thought about the things that the detectives had put in the evidence room down in the basement. He decided that perhaps he should have another look. Maybe something was missed. Maybe Smith and Crane had overlooked something, then again, maybe I did, who knows. *It never hurts to look one last time, especially when your mind is fresh*, he thought.

"Lupe," he said.

"Yes, Charlie," she said, looking up from her paperwork.

"I'm going to be gone for a few minutes. Would you watch my desk for me and answer my phone? Please."

"Sure, Charlie."

"Thanks, kid, remind me I owe you a dinner will you? For all the nice things you do for me, that is."

"Can I bring a date, Charlie?" she said, then she grinned.

"Hell, why not," he said. "You're worth that much and more."

"You're sweet, Charlie."

"Yeah, well, tell that to anyone and the date's off."

"Gotcha. Not a word," she said. Then she slipped over to his desk and started typing up her paperwork.

Charlie traveled down the hall; it seemed unusually busy for a weeknight. Barnie was smashed and so was his girlfriend Rose and the booze was reeking from their bodies. They were not maneuvering too well down the hall. Both looked like they had been through World War II with the cuts and bruises on their faces. "Fighting again?" he asked.

Terman said, "That isn't the half of it with these two. She was mad at the dog, the dog was chasing the bull, Barnie was trying to close the gate. Then the dog decided he would chase the cat. That tripped Rose, Barnie was screaming at her, she hit him and he hit her back and when we got there they were both naked and rolling around in the mud." Terman just shook his head. "When will they ever learn? These two will kill each other if they don't stop drinking."

Charlie just laughed and headed down the stairs. The evidence room was located way past several small offices at the end of the hall. There were boxes upon boxes stacked that had been labeled, dated, and categorized. Chuck Benson was in charge and he expected that everyone follow his rules. "What can I do for you today, Charlie?"

"Well, I was kind of looking over the facts in the Gannon murder and I was hoping you would let me see the contents of her box. You know, everything from the accident on down."

"You will have to sign in. Not everything is tagged on that, I'm still working on some of it, so don't be lifting any evidence to take out with you."

"No," said Charlie, "I just want a look and maybe take a picture or two?"

"I don't know about that, Charlie. Maybe, that's not a real good idea."

"Okay. Well, can I see it?"

"It's number 47. I'll take the box and set it on the table and you can look through it. You signed in, didn't you?" Then he set the box down on the table.

"Sure did, Chuck, name and hour and date."

Charlie carefully looked through the box. Inside there were pieces of Mary's purse, driver's license, a couple of credit cards, money: two tens and one hundred dollar bill, two bottles of whiskey one half full, a lighter, a pack of mangled smokes and a fancy bracelet. He took each item and looked at them carefully, turning them over and over. Then he picked up the bracelet and slowly rolled it over in his hand. Something caught his eye. "Hey, Chuck! Do you have a magnifying glass?"

"Sure, there's one in the top of my desk on the right. Did you find something?"

"No," said Charlie, "it's just my eyes. They don't always see just right."

"Yeah, it's called an age thing, Charlie," said Chuck, laughing.

Charlie rolled it over again in his fingers. He could make out some of the initials; Charlie squinted, pulling the magnifying glass closer to get a better look. He looked around to see if Chuck was watching him. He was busy at the window talking to Bob. Charlie took advantage of this and pulled out his tiny camera. He took pictures of the bracelet, one front and back and one as close as he could get on the lettering. Then he quickly slipped it back into his pocket. Charlie looked around at Bob and Chuck. They were in a warm debate over the rules. Charlie left the box and its contents on the table, then he pulled the sign out sheet to him, putting his ID and time out on it.

Chuck looked at him, "Did you find anything interesting?"

Bobs' eyebrows went up and he hollered, "Chuck, will you pay attention? I need to place these things in a box on the inside."

"No, Chuck," said Charlie, "just the same ole same ole stuff, nothing new really." When he started up the stairs he could still hear them arguing. Then he heard Chuck open the door, "Just this once," he said, "and I'll let you. Now get off my back, will ya?"

Charlie decided the best way to handle this was to take a few of those days he had coming before he retired. *This way,* he thought, *I won't draw attention to what I'm doing or any suspicion.* He knocked on Jeff's door.

"Come in," he said.

He popped his head in and asked, "Say, you have anything going on for me this week, from about today through next Thursday?"

Jeff thought for a moment. "No not really, Charlie, are you taking vacation time?"

"Yes, you could say that. Anyway, I have some time coming and I thought I might as well take some of it before I retire. That is, if that's okay with you and you don't mind?"

"Hey, no problem, go ahead, enjoy your time off," he said.

With that taken care of, Charlie left Jeff's office and headed out. He took the film out of his camera and drove over to Jesse's house. He told him that it was real important that all the pictures where clear and enlarged. "I need a close up shot," he stressed to him. "Please don't screw this up, bud. These are all I have of them."

Jesses nodded his head. "How long before you need them?"

"Yesterday," said Charlie.

"It figures," he said. "I'll have them ready for you bright and early in the morning." Then he shut his door behind Charlie.

Charlie slept good that night, even with dreams of the bracelet. The initials kept running and rerunning through his mind. When he woke up, his house was silent. Only the ticking of his old clock echoed in his bedroom. He rubbed his eyes trying to get the sleepies out of them. The walls of his bedroom long ago were badly in need of paint; they were a smoky green. The curtains were rotting through where the sun had hit every day all afternoon. Charlie slid his feet to the floor and sat on the edge of his bed. *Why do I keep this old place?* he thought. *It's about as depressing a place as I've ever seen. My dresser is a mess; I can't find anything, only one handle to pull out the drawers with.* He reached for the chair next to his bed and picked up his pants. *One foot, one leg at a time,* he told himself. Soon he was dressed. He grabbed his wallet and looked inside. *Not much in there,* he thought to himself. *I need to go by the bank before I leave.* He put extra clothes in the duffle bag, grabbed his keys and locked the door behind him.

Jesse had the pictures ready and waiting when Charlie arrived at 4:48 a.m. "So what's so important, Charlie, was it the initials on it?" he said, grinning from ear to ear.

"So let me see them," said Charlie and Jesse laughed. He handed him the pictures. "These are good, Jesse, real good, nice, clean, just what I wanted," he said with a big smile.

"I only do the best you know," said Jesse proudly.

"That's why I come to you and only you," he said as he left, letting the door slam behind him. "Thanks again," he said.

Charlie had put in a call to the Gannon ranch on his way out of town. Rich told him to come on out, that he and Jake were up anyway. Sitting in his old car he thumbed through the pictures. He was excited as he turned the key and drove off to the ranch. When he arrived, the lights in the house were shining out brightly through the windows. He went through the gate, up the steps, and knocked on the front door. He stood there for a few minutes looking around, whistling to himself.

"Come on in, Charlie," said Jake. "We have a fresh pot of coffee just perked, would you like a cup?"

"I sure would, hmmmm, something smells wonderful," he said, sniffing the air.

"Hey, how about some chow too? We have plenty you know, are you hungry?"

"Yes, I am but are you sure you have enough?" he said.

"Yeah, come on in, we have plenty, we'll fix you right up," said Jake, then he closed the door behind them. Charlie and Jake had been friends for a long time. They gone to the same school together, enlisted in the army at the same time, and had been good steady friends for many years. Only Jake took on the country style and Charlie, well, he preferred more of the brighter lights. The difference between them never seemed to matter. When Charlie, who was the bigger eater of the two, had finished every bite he could find and Jake had poured him another cup of coffee, he looked at Charlie, smiling broadly, he said, "Can I get you anything else?"

"No." He patted his belly with both hands. "I don't think I can hold another bite, but thanks anyway."

Jake asked, "Okay, Charlie. What brings you, business or pleasure?"

"A little of both you two. Have you seen Crane and Smith yet?"

"Yes," said Rich, "they where here yesterday asking questions. Some of them really ticked me off."

"Well," said Charlie, "I knew they were coming, I just didn't know when. Anyway, don't ask me any questions just now, but let me ask you a few if you don't mind, then maybe I can clear this situation a bit." Charlie pulled out of his briefcase all the pictures except five. He laid them out on the table and Rich picked them up and started looking.

"Hey, that's the bracelet that Mary took when she ran away," said Rich.

"Did you buy it for her?" asked Charlie

"No, actually, I didn't. She told me she bought it for herself. In fact, she kept it behind her jewelry box most of the time."

"Didn't you find that was a bit odd?" asked Charlie.

"Well no, Mary did a lot of things that were odd. And so that was not really out of her character."

"Okay. Well, that's all I need for now," and he pushed himself away from the table. "I have a lot of footwork ahead of me so, guys, thanks for the breakfast. I'll get back to you on this when I know more myself." He thanked them again for the chow and headed down the road.

He drove the shortest distance of all the surrounding towns he had to go in hopes that finding his information would be one of those easy first timers. No such luck, the stores not only had not ever seen the bracelet, they told him it had to be a special order, one of a kind. So Charlie grabbed a snack and headed for K Falls, one-hundred miles away. He spent most of the day going from store to store, shopping malls, main street stores, he finally gave in and decided to get a motel and spend the night. No one knew anything about the bracelet. Charlie was feeling discouraged. He had hoped for better results. In the morning, he climbed into his old car and headed out the highway on 97 toward Bend. He began all over again, going from shop to shop. *I know I'm right,* he thought, *I just have to prove it.* He had only two hours left before the stores closed, so he went ahead and booked a room at an old motel, then he headed for the downtown area. It was the old part of the town that had been renovated and redone. Mostly it seemed to belong to the yuppies and their inner circle of friends. They all chatted and stayed in the general area of the shops there, as if they were the only existing people on earth and it belonged solely to them. He found the old jewelry shop on the corner. It had the aura of a Santa's shop with twinkle lights blinking on and off. The window held felt boxes of diamond rings. Some matched the necklaces as sets. Some were blue sapphires, and there were rubies and all glittered brightly. He could see through the window on the wall the old cuckoo clocks and the old white haired man behind the counter. The bell jingled as Charlie stepped through the door.

"Hello, can I help you, sir?" asked the proprietor

"Yes," said Charlie, and he pulled out his photos. "I'm really kinda out of my district, but I'm looking for the person who could have, or may have designed or made this bracelet, or one like it." And then he laid the photos on the counter.

"Yes," he said slowly "...I recognize this piece. I did this one myself," he said proudly. "It was a special order for a gentleman, as I recall. It was being made for a very special lady and he was very specific about how he wanted it to look," he said.

"Did he give the lady's name?"

"No, didn't say," he said frowning. He shook his head then scratching his hair he squinted his eyes as if to reach way back into his memories. Then, as if a light bulb had come on, he said, "But I have a receipt for that exact bracelet and I know it would have his name on it. Would you like a copy of that?"

"I sure would," said Charlie.

The old guy left him for a few moments and sat at his old rolled top desk. He opened one of his drawers and Charlie could see that he had receipts after receipts. *He'll never find it in that mess,* he thought.

But to his surprise the old man pulled it out and said, "Here it is. I thought I knew right where it was."

Before he could hand it to him, Charlie pulled out all his pictures. "Would you mind taking a look at these?" Then he laid all his pictures down on the counter. "I have several of them here."

The old man pushed his glasses back on his face and squinted his eyes looking very carefully at each one. "Do you recognize anyone, sir?"

"Oh yes," and he pointed to one of the pictures. "That's him all right. This one right here."

Charlie smiled. *Gotcha!* he thought to himself. When he left the shop, he had all the evidence he needed to get a confession. His stomach was growling and he remembered the one thing that hadn't changed in the downtown area was Eddies. It was the best Chinese food in town. Besides, the company there was always good. He finally retired to his room and sorted out his paperwork. Tomorrow he was going to head home and have a serious talk with the sheriff. He was going to blow the town away. He had the murderer dead to rights. He closed his eyes as he slid into the fresh sheets. *These sure do feel good,* he thought, then before he knew it he was out like a light.

Chapter Forty-Eight

When Charlie had left them and went on his trip, the two men, Rich and Jake decided to clear the dishes, putting them in the sink and get themselves back to the outside ranch work.

"I hired Maria to come over and clean this place up," said Rich.

Jake frowned, trying to remember who she was. "You know her," said Rich, "She's Ole Mex's daughter, only you think of her as a little six-year-old girl."

Jake smiled. "Oh yeah, I remember her now. You had her here about a year ago, she did a real fine job. And by the way, are you trying to tell me I'm getting old."

"No," said Rich, grinning. "You just looked like you didn't know who she was."

"Well, I guess I did forget for a moment," he said, then Jake's voice got real quiet. "We need to talk, Rich. I think, well, we have time for…" then he said, "Let's have another cup of coffee, okay?" Jake waved his hand toward the chair indicating for Rich to sit down. "I know we have chores to do, but what I have to say won't take long and I'd like your full attention if I might."

"Okay," he said and he pulled up a chair, "this sounds serious."

"I don't know if you know it or not as yet, but Bess went home last night. Sally got her there just fine. She's a still a little weak, the doctor says, but she will be okay. I, ahmm, Sally told me you were there every night except last night when no one was around. You slipped into her room and stayed most of the night keeping watch over her."

"No. I didn't know she went home. I guess I should have gone so I could have taken her home. Is there a problem with me being there by her side?"

"No, not really. I just wanted you to know I'm glad that you did. I'm glad you were there for her," he said, letting out a sigh. "But what I wanted to tell you is that last night after Sally got Bess home and settled in she had a visitor."

"Who?" said Rich bristling.

"Well, try this one on for size. Your mother-in-law, no less."

"What? Why would she go there?"

"Well, as Sally related it to me, she had two letters. One for Bess, and one she had opened that was for her. It seems the old guy," and then Jake closed his eyes for a moment thinking back in time, he said, "and I do remember the time way back," shaking his head, "when he had an affair with a real doozy of a floozy years ago. Anyway, during that time your mother-in-law had suspected she knew what was going on with him. So, being friends with Bess's dad for years, she decided that the lady herself would have a one time fling, hoping it would wake old Wesley up, and it did just that. Bess's pa always had a thing for Deanie, so it was an easy enough thing for her to do I guess, and when it was all over with, both the Harlows decided that they had messed up pretty bad. Only Wesley, you see, was the only one between them both who knew both sides of the story. Deanie didn't know that when Wesley had his little fling, that the old girl got knocked up. Well, two babies were conceived, and believe it or not, on the same night. One was Bess, and Deanie was, and is really her mom…"

Rich stood up. "WHAT! This is unreal," he said.

"Yeah, well, sit down here and let me tell you all about it. Here's how the rest of the story goes. Both women went into labor the same night and both babies were born. You can say for sure old Wesley was sweating up a storm over that one. He found out that night Jessie didn't want anything to do with that kid she just gave birth to, so old Wesley put up big money to have them babies switched right then and there."

"How did he know Bess wasn't his?" he asked.

"That's a good question. Well, according to his letter it was because he hadn't been with Deanie at any time during that period of time. He talked Bess's dad into raising her, only Bess's dad thought all along he was raising Wesley's daughter from the floozy."

"Boy, talk about complicated."

"Sure is," said Jake, "and so Deanie, then, was thinking she was pregnant with a child from old Wess. Only Bess's Dad had started to suspect the real possibilities about all this just before he had his heart attack. The old man had been paying him for years to keep what was rightfully his anyway."

"That explains his last phone call to Bess," said Rich thinking back

"Well, I guess they had met that day and argued about it. He had told Wess he had invested every penny for her and it was in stocks put away in a locked vault with letters and the key, and was in one of the boxes in the house somewhere. They got into such a heated argument that her dad began having chest pains and Wesley just stood by and didn't bother to help him. He said in his letter how sorry he was now that he thought at the time letting him die was the answer to his prayers, and so he just stood there while her dad died, but not before he had begged old Wess to tell his daughter how much he loved her after all these years, and that somehow he always knew."

"That's a lot for anyone to digest all once," Rich said, frowning.

"If that ain't a fact," said Jake

"How did she take all that?" said Rich, raising his eyebrows.

"Well, how would you swallow it?"

"Yeah, I know that was a real dumb statement."

"Well, in answer to your question, Sally said not very well. Said that she sobbed uncontrollably and it was difficult to get her to stop." Jake's fingers were picking at the loose paint on his chair, it was hard for him to look Rich in the eye. He felt a lot of anger toward old Wess.

"It seems my family one way or the other is hell bent on destroying her. You know that, Jake?" Jake was silent. Rich got up. Slipping his hands into his pockets, he walked to the window and stared out at the barn, his vision a blur. "So why did Deanie tell her now, for Christ sake? Why not wait until Mary was buried?"

"She was there for forgiveness, Rich," he said quietly. "She felt she had been party to all Bess' troubles AND she also told her she knew about the love that you two had for each other."

"NO! Oh God, no!" he said, wiping his forehead. He was feeling sick for both of them. "How in the hell, Jake, did she find out? Who told her?" His voice raised he turned around to face him.

"You know you can't keep things like that quiet in a small town like this. Besides, does it really matter now? I don't think so," he said quietly. "Anyway, she was on a peace mission and she asked to get to know her daughter in the future, maybe when time had healed things for them both. She also handed Bess a certified check in Bess's name for, now get this, one-million dollars."

"What? You've got to be kidding me. Why? How come? That's a lot of money."

"Slow down, son. I know what you're thinking. I was shocked too. I guess old Wesley had left it to her, to Bess, in his will and she cannot give it back, it's irrevocable. That's the stipulation. It was not to be put back into his estate. I believe the old guy was trying to make amends for what he had done. Not once in Bess's lifetime, but twice. And damn straight that's a lot of money, but apparently he felt he owed it to her."

"That's a lot to digest even for me. I can't imagine what it must be like for her."

"Well, she just kind of sat there I guess, and then she told Deanie she couldn't think right now and she wished she would leave. Deanie said she understood, that she had a funeral, in fact two funerals to plan, anyway. So that being beside the point, she hoped that when and if she was ever ready to talk about all this, please pick up the phone and call."

"Maybe I should go to her, Jake, what do you think?"

"Well, I think with Sally there and Juanita, Mex's other girl, that Bess is better left alone right now. She has enough help and, besides, seeing you will only remind her she has lost the baby and I personally don't think she needs this right now."

"Yeah, maybe you're right," he said, "but I'm not waiting very long, I can tell you that."

"Come on," said Jake, "we have a ton of things to do around this joint." He got up and headed for the door. "It will be nice to have Maria over to clean this place up. It's beginning to smell like two bachelors live here."

"Yeah, it does," said Rich. "This afternoon I'm going to Deanies to visit with the kids and see how they are doing. After the funeral I'm bringing them home, Jake. They have been away from home for far too long. I don't know what I was thinking when I left them there so long. I'm no better than Mary when it comes to taking care of them. I should have brought them home sooner."

"I agree," said Jake. "They need to be with you now more than ever."

"Well, Maria is going to get their rooms ready today and then she's going to stay on for awhile. I like to get her as a permanent housekeeper and nanny if she will."

"She might," he said. "She's real good. Now how about we get this work done. We can talk all we want while we finish. There's a calf down in the lower field, Rich, I want you to look at," said Jake as he closed the door behind them and they headed for the barn.

Chapter Forty-Nine

The trip back for Charlie was going be strictly pleasure. He had sailed to Bend in such a hurry, and his mind had been crowded with so many facts that Charlie had not taken notice of the view. *It was beautiful country, that was for sure,* he thought to himself. *But nothing like when I grew up here, a lot has changed.* Charlie was born in Bend, at the St. Charles Memorial hospital many years ago. It no longer existed on the hill any more, because of a thing called progress that had consumed the town. He headed out of the big city with the knowledge that his task was almost at an end. He remembered as he traveled the thirty-mile trip with his folks to LaPine that it had always seemed to take forever as a child.

Passing Lava Butte he wondered at the beauty of such a volcanic rock. It blended so well with the tall pines and the busy traffic as his car clunked alongside the fast pace of the four-lane highway passing the butte. Approaching the small town of LaPine, he thought about the store his mom always stopped at when he was a kid. She would stop and buy a slice or one-quarter pound of the sharp cheddar cheese they had on their counter in a round brick. It was her favorite, and he remembered her mouth would almost drool as she stood at the counter to pay for it. He couldn't have been very old at the time he thought as he could just barely see over the counter. Years later, when his mom was dying from cancer and he was a mere boy of twenty, he had stopped in and paid for a slice, or to be precise, a quarter pound of the cheddar cheese in the round brick. But to search his memory he couldn't remember if she ate any of it or was able to ever eat it. It was just too long ago. He didn't like to think of those times of his youth too much, as it still had the sting of lost hugs and empty spaces that couldn't be touched again. *Besides, it hurt too much,* he thought. He wasn't sure if the store was still there or not anymore. He hadn't really looked and his thoughts wouldn't let him go there.

Charlie turned off at the sign stating Lakeview 144 miles. He was glad to get out of the heavy traffic as the highway had become a death trap for many, as it could no longer hold all who traveled on it. He used to enjoy the next trek of this trip when he was younger, but environmentalists had interfered so much with lawsuits and such that the forests were dying and brown. Charlie had no use for those people and he wasn't afraid to say so. Oh, he was as careful as the next fellow, and he did his share of recycling of his garbage, and that included when he visited the outdoors as well. He only used what he needed and never disturbing what god had intended for all to be enjoyed, but he felt strongly about the people that called themselves environmentalists. They were usually the ones who lived in the east who sat behind the desks. They thought they knew more about how to tell us how to run our forests than we who have lived in the west all our lives. They were paper chasers and shit stirrers and lawsuit fanatics. He strongly felt that the people who seemed to think they knew all the answers here were in fact destroying the beautiful forests themselves, all in the name of their lawsuit. It was a power trip. *But no matter*, thought Charlie. *You can't fight those with plenty of money to spend.*

He drove passed Fort Rock, only encountering an occasional car here and there. This was sagebrush country, sand and juniper. Oh how he loved the smell of juniper. *Nothing like it*, he thought, *when you sawed through the wood or burned it in a fireplace.* The smell was indescribable. Before Charlie knew it he had passed Silver Lake, Summer Lake and was heading out of Paisley. *Boy, it will be good to get back home, even to that rat hole I call home.*

Charlie had never married; he couldn't seem to get the hang of the relationship thing down pat. He didn't know how to let someone into his life, when people got to close to him he would push them away. He had been a loner all of his life. The closest one he had ever let near him was Jake, and even at that he was cautious about it. *Here I am, almost home,* he thought, as he noticed the six mile mark. Soon he was unloading his car, packing his bag and briefcase into the house.

Tomorrow, he thought. *Yes, tomorrow I'm having a long talk with the sheriff. But tonight it's a hot shower for this old boy, a cold beer and maybe take in some tube. Or,* he thought to himself, *maybe just plain crawl into bed.* He was tired after his long trip. *It was worth it,* he thought as he took one last sip of his beer. He slipped into the sheets on his bed and Charlie was out like a light.

The night sky sparkled with stars here and there, but it began to cloud up like a rain was on its way. Nothing moved as the quiet set in the house and around Charlie. Only the occasional moan and groan could be heard and the creaking of the house as it settled in for the night.

Chapter Fifty

"Hi," she said softly, "how are you?"

"I'm fine," he said. "I just wanted to call and see. Well, the question is, how are you doing?"

"You sound tired, Richard," she said, avoiding the question.

"Not really, I'll be fine. So please don't worry about me."

"You know, Sally told me that you stayed with me every night while I was in the hospital. I wish you hadn't done that, you know. Richard, people are talking, they are whispering."

"Bethleen," he said, sighing and looking around the room, "I really don't care what they are saying. It's none of their damn business."

"When is Deanie going to have the funerals?" she said quietly, changing the subject.

"Tomorrow. Bethleen, I don't want to talk about that right now. I wanted you to know how I am sorry about the baby." He was at a loss for words, he didn't know how to fill the silence that was between them. *And what do I know about the pain she's feeling?* he said to himself. *I only know she's hurting real bad and I need to let her know how much I care.* "I'm so very sorry," he said. He just didn't know what else to say.

"It'll be okay," she said. "For whatever reason, it wasn't meant to be." She cried softly so he couldn't hear. "I have to go now," she said, wiping her nose on her sleeve. "Thanks for calling." And she carefully set the phone down on the receiver.

Rich listened as the phone clicked lightly and the dial tone wined in his ear. He stood frozen, letting the phone slowly slide down his chest. He was lost in the moment and his thoughts were numb. He woke out of his dream-like state with a start, slamming the phone down on the receiver.

I know, he thought, *I know.* He felt a sense of panic and began to run, leaving the house in such a hurry he left the door open. He headed for the barn, he needed Jake and he needed him right now.

Chapter Fifty-One

Bess couldn't see through the tears. Her body slumped and she fell to the floor sobbing. Her mind felt numb, so confused. She thought she heard music from the radio, it didn't make any sense. It felt like she had been crying for days, *Or was it years,* she thought, she didn't know. When she tried to focus on the room, it just stayed blurry. *Was the phone ringing? No, it can't be. I can't talk now, can't deal with anymore. Who's razor is this? Where did it come from? I've got to move; my body feels so heavy. Oh, I don't want to be here. Don't want to be here any more at all.* She sobbed. *Richard, where did you come from?* She thought. *You want the razor? Okay, it's just a dream anyway,* she said sobbing, *just a dream, only a dream.* She closed her eyes as the tears flowed down her face.

"No, it's not a dream, little one," he said as he lifted her up into his arms. He kissed her face tenderly. "I'll never leave you again. You won't ever have to fight any more battles alone." He sat down in the rocker holding her so close he could feel her breath. He rocked her until she was sound asleep, then he slipped her into her gown and pulled back the covers and tucked her in. It had been dark a long time now. Rich turned out all the lights in the house, locked the doors, leaving the music playing on the radio. He climbed into the bed beside her and pulled her close. "I'll never let you down again, little one," he whispered, brushing his fingers through her hair. He closed his eyes as he kissed her forehead gently. The music played softly throughout the house, then the tittering and tattering could be heard as the new spring rain fell cleansing the souls that lay asleep in the night.

Chapter Fifty-Two

Jeff was tired, and so he piled up his papers, shut off the computer, putting everything away, cleaning up and wiping things off. He grabbed his keys and was about to walk out the door when his phone buzzed.

"I really hate to bother you," said Bob, "but we have another one on the line."

"Another one what?" said Jeff

"Complaint against our guys," said Bob. "They have managed to tick this man off big time, he's really hot under the collar."

Scratching his head, Jeff thought, *How many of these complaints have I taken today, I've lost count.* "Okay, put him through," he said, sighing.

Jeff talked to the guy for better than an hour explaining to him how important this investigation was and that finding the person who did murder Mary, and stopping them was a number one priority and they really could use his help. If he was able to even remember anything, just anything, no matter how small it might seem, or ordinary, it could mean the difference between getting the killer and letting them go. And, besides, he told him, if you're telling the truth you don't have anything to worry about. He told him he would appreciate it if he would let it pass this time the way his investigators had handled this situation with him in view of the fact that they would be answering to him personally anyway. He said to him "We are working very hard on analyzing all the information in this case and looking under every rock trying to uncover all the facts. We hope to have a big break in this soon."

Well, the guy decided Jeff might be right, so he backed down and apologized to him, saying maybe he had just jumped the gun. Jeff told him it was okay, everyone is entitled to their own opinion, and a murder in a small town like this only makes everyone nervous. He was glad the man had decided to cooperate and he told him so. He said that citizens such as himself should be commended for coming forth. They agreed no hard feeling and decided to let it all drop. The man thanked Jeff for his time and understanding.

"That's no problem," he said. "That's what I'm here for," and he hung up the phone. He wiped the perspiration from his brow. He thought to himself, *That was a bit of smart public relations*, as he patted himself on the back, then he thought that could have just as easily turned into a nasty nightmare. *Phewwww.*

When the light went out on Jeff's phone, it was the signal Bob needed to pop in and talk to the sheriff. He wanted in on this investigation and this seemed to be the opportune time to catch him alone. "Say, Jeff, you got a moment?"

"Why sure, I can go out that door anytime, come on in. What can I do for you?"

"Well, I kind of would like, well, you see…shit!" he said, moaning.

"Spit it out there, Bob," said Jeff, grinning.

"I was wondering how the investigation is going?" he said, fidgeting in his seat.

"Well, Krandell finished the autopsies and sent the bodies to the morgue just awhile ago and I understand the funerals are in the afternoon tomorrow at three. Other than that, I don't have all the paperwork on it as yet, why?"

"Well, you know I'm working on taking my detective test. I would really just like more hands on with the cases that we have going on here so I can better myself, and this one is as good as any to start with."

"Well, Bob, there's nothing wrong with that. Hold that thought, Bob while I get this call. Will this day ever end," he said as he punched the line. "Yes," he said as he began tapping his pencil on his desk. "Okay, Lupe, I'll take it."

"Hi, Krandell. The preliminary. Okay…okay…hmmmm, that's very interesting. Anything else? What kind? Yes, I'll pick that up then. I appreciate it. Have a good night, and thanks for staying so late for me to finish this." Hanging up the phone, he noticed Bob fidgeting. Frowning, he said, "Something wrong with you, Bob?"

"No, nothing, just didn't remember you tapping with the pencil before and it's one of my pet peeves. It drives me up the wall. It's like hearing someone scratch on a chalkboard, it hurts the ears. Sorry about that."

As he laid the pencil down, he grinned and said, "No problem, it's an old habit I have. It helps me to think."

"Did you find anything out?" he said, sounding anxious and excited. "That was the coroner, right?"

"Yes, it was, but I'm not going to deal with any of this until I get all the paperwork put together. Anyway, it's late. Tell you what, Bob, how about you come in around 9:00 in the morning and I'll brief you on everything we have so far."

"Well, Jeff, I want to, but I have something important that needs attending to and I really can't get out of it."

"Sure, would 11:00 be better for you?"

"Yes, I'll be back to town by then. I sure do appreciate this."

"Great, I'll get together with Smith and Crane and we'll meet in my office here. Then if we need more room, we can lay everything out in the interrogation room." He smiled. "We'll make it our conference room okay?"

Bob smiled. "Thanks, Jeff. I'll see you then, I'm going to head home now. I'm tired and I have a long day ahead of me tomorrow."

After Bob had left the building, Jeff received two more calls. One from the man who had been so hot earlier that it took time to convince him to calm down. He had remembered something he said. It didn't seem odd at the time, and maybe it wasn't really important. When he had been talking to Jeff earlier, he hadn't thought it worth mentioning until he thought it over, and when he remembered that Jeff had said no matter how small for him to call. So, as that good citizen, here he was with what he saw. The other phone call one was from Chuck, and something was amiss in the evidence room. He had some information pertaining to the case.

"My, My, MY," said Jeff, "this is getting more interesting by the minute." He locked everything up, did his last minute dust job, and decided that tonight for a change he would lock his door as well. It was one of those gut feelings he would get every now and then.

Jeff decided his bed tonight would feel real good to him. He wondered what tomorrow would bring. It would be interesting to say the least. The trip home had been a fast one, and as he pulled into his driveway he thought he had seen a shadow in the back yard near his fence. He left the lights on his pickup and grabbed his flashlight, heading around the other side of the house. He crept carefully, looking with his light, shining it around the brush and under the hedge near the flowers, taking great care to lift things as he went.

The tool shed out back was small, but Jeff shined his light on and around it anyway. He didn't see anything, so he decided that he was just jumpy after his long day and some of the information he had gotten. He shut the lights off in his rig, locked the door and headed for the house.

I need to call Sarah, he thought as he went through his door, locking it behind him. Jeff reached into his refrigerator and pulled out a beer. He sat down in the recliner, popped open the can, and picked up the phone. He dialed her number. He told Sarah he was way too tired to come over tonight. Jeff asked her about her day and how she was feeling. They chitchatted for about an hour when he told her he missed her, that he would get with her tomorrow, and to have a good night.

After he hung up, Jeff headed for his shower. The water running over his back felt so good to him, relieving the tension in his neck and back. He stayed in there for twenty minutes letting it soothe his soul. Jeff wrapped the towel around himself and took one more check on all the doors and windows, making sure all was locked up tight. He pulled back his blankets and sat on the bed winding his clock for an early morning rise.

It's raining, he thought, *coming down pretty good.* He crawled in and pulled the covers up around his shoulders, closing his eyes to the world. *Tomorrow,* he thought, *tomorrow...* and he was soon in a deep sleep.

The rain poured down, soaking the ground, covering the tracks that had been made in the mud. The key fit in the door and unlocked it, opening it without any trouble or sound. The rain beat down even harder, drowning out all around it. Another key popped open the briefcase that sat on the table, and papers were sifted through with the use of a small light.

"Damn it!" was the whisper. Then everything was thrown back in the case and it was quietly shut. The light went from room to room, and drawer to drawer. Then it slipped out the door, leaving in its wake muddy prints on the floor. The rain poured even more, letting those that slept within hear only the chattering of the drops that banged on the roof, and a sleep so peaceful the waking would not come until the drizzle of the morning dawn.

Chapter Fifty-Three

Sally wondered about the call she had gotten from Jake. He sounded edgy and wasn't offering any information. Sometimes he could be evasive and not tell all, keeping things to himself, as if he were he to speak the world would end in a big boom. She would just have to read between the lines. Tonight when she hung up the phone she knew he was keeping something from her. She just felt it and wanted to know why. She paced the floor, wondering what she should do. It was late and the rains had come. They were soaking the earth, causing small rivers to flow in the culverts outside.

I think my only answers lie in talking to Jake face to face, she thought. So Sally grabbed up her coat and hat and slid her hand into the strap on her umbrella. She turned out her kitchen light and locked the door. Sally was soaked by the time she reached her car. The wind had caught her umbrella and turned it inside out.

"A lot of help you are, you stupid rain stick," she mumbled to herself. "Now I'm soaked to the bone." She threw it on the ground, off to the side of her car and slid into the seat. When she turned the key, her old car whined, the starter just barely turning over, then it caught and the engine roared. As she backed out of her driveway, she turned on the lights and her heater. She was suddenly chilled to the bone.

The trip didn't take long, and soon she was pulling up in front of the house. Sally turned off the car, slammed the door shut, and ran for the back of the house to the kitchen where she saw the lights were on. She stood under the eve of the door and knocked. Jake saw her through the window and hurried to the door, unlocking it. He had a surprised look on his face, as Sally had not said anything about coming out, and especially at this hour.

"Sally, what are you doing here?" he asked. "You're going to catch your death of cold," he said as he helped her take off her drenched coat and hung it to dry.

"I'm really sorry, Jake. I wouldn't bother you normally at this hour, but I felt like you weren't telling me all there was to tell about Bess and I got concerned," she said, pulling her dripping wet hair back and pining it back up on her head.

"Here, let's get you out of those wet clothes and next to the fire, then we'll talk." He put his arm around her and gently walked her to the bottom of the stairs in the living room. "You'll find a robe in the first bedroom at the top of the stairs, Sal. It's in the closet next to the bath. Let's get you out of those wet things and them into the dryer, and then we can talk. Okay?"

"Thanks, Jake."

Sally changed into Rich's robe in the upstairs bedroom. She hadn't realized she was so wet until her cloths began to stick to her body as she took them off. She set her wet clothes up one by one on the chair to be taken down and thrown into the dryer, then slipping into the blue robe, she wrapped it around her small frame and hollered down to Jake, "Are you sure he won't mind me wearing this?"

"No," Jake said as he hollered back. "Mary bought it for him and he never liked it, so it's like brand-new. Besides, robes aren't his style, as you ladies would put it." Then he laughed.

"I'm just about done, I'll be down in a minute," she said as she put a comb through her hair. She had let her hair out of the tight bun she always wore and left it hanging loose.

"Would you like a cup of coffee?" he asked from the bottom of the stairs.

"Yes, Jake, that would be nice. That would taste real good," she said as she descended the stairs.

He put his hand gently on her back and escorted her to a chair in the kitchen. He took her clothes, stepped around the corner, and threw them into the dryer. Then he returned to the kitchen, and picking up the coffee pot, he poured Sally and himself a cup.

She sat looking at him with gentle wonderment in her eyes. "Jake, are you going to tell me what's going on? Please, you sounded so evasive on the phone."

"I like it when you wear your hair down, Sal. It adds to your beauty."

"Thank you, Jake, but please don't change the subject. I'm worried."

"Okay! Okay!" he said, raising his hands. "This afternoon Rich and I were working on the barn. We've had some repairs to do on account of all the storms. Anyway, Rich went up to the house to call Bess and see how things were going. He wanted to know how she was feeling and to let her know he was going to come over after the funerals tomorrow whether she liked it or not. The next thing I knew he was running like a banshee down to the barn and he hollers at me 'Bess is alone and something's wrong, something's real wrong with her,' he says. 'I tried calling her back, but she wouldn't answer.' We both had thought that someone was staying with her, Sal, but he said he was sure she was alone and he didn't like her state of mind, and that she had hung up on him."

"Oh, my gosh, Jake. She told me…she said she would be fine, that's, that's what she said. She convinced both Juanita and I that she would be all right. So we left."

"Now don't you go a blamin' yourself, Sal. I won't have it," said Jake, patting her back. "Anyway, so he took off out of here, peeling out with the truck like he was on a racetrack. I thought he would wreck the truck before he got there. Anyway, I guess it's a good thing he did as it turns out. He called me back later and said he had found her on the floor. She had a razor in her hand. And she was out of it, didn't recognize much of anything around her. He said her eyes were glazed."

Sally gasped, "Oh, my God! Is she okay, Jake?"

"Yes," he said, "but Rich doesn't know if she intended to use it, but he took it away from her and managed to get her settled in some. Finally she fell sound asleep and then he tucked her into bed. He called the doctor to see if there was anything else he could do. He told him about her condition and how he thought the life had just gone right out of her, that there wasn't too many sparks left in her. The doctor said that his office had tried to call earlier and hadn't got any response from it. They had some news they wanted to share with her that they thought might help her mental state.

"What could possibly help her in this state?" asked Sally

"Well, Sal, I guess Bess is still pregnant."

"What? How can that be? She lost the baby, right?" she asked.

"Well," said Jake. "I guess the story is she was carrying twins, and one of them survived. Somehow that had got past the doctor the first time. You know, doctors are human too, and they make mistakes. I guess they had taken more tests in the hospital just before she was released to make sure she was okay, and that's what they found after she left. Well, anyway, you know what I'm talking about," he said blushing. He picked up his cup and sipped it.

"Yes, I know what you're saying, Jake, so go on."

"He said the Doc wanted her to get all the sleep she could now and to watch her close in case she was having any more ideas about suicide, if indeed that was her plan to begin with. Then Rich asked me if I would get his clothes and bring them over in the morning so he could dress for the funerals there.

I said, 'Sure, anything else you need?' He told me, 'Yes, could I help him find someone to stay with her while he went to the funerals?" Well Sally, I have tried everywhere and they are all going to be there at the funerals tomorrow. I haven't been able to come up with a single soul who is free. Have you got any ideas? Someone you know who you can call?"

"Yes," she said, "ME." She reached over and covered his hand with hers.

"Sally," he said, squeezing her little fingers, "I figured you wanted to be there tomorrow, so I didn't even think about asking you."

"Well, that's what you get for not asking or thinking," she said, indignant. "It isn't imperative that I be there. I have already made up my dish to take for after the funeral and my sympathy card is ready to go. So if you take them for me, that's really all that matters anyway, isn't it? I know Deanie will understand and, besides, it's far more important that we take care of the living then the dead. Besides, you know I love that girl as much as if she were my own, or if you don't, you should."

"I know you do," he said.

"It's settled then. I'll stay with her," she said, pouring herself another cup of coffee.

"I'm sure Rich will appreciate that, Sal, I know I do. Excuse me, hon. I'll be right back."

He left her sitting at the table. Sally took the quiet moments and stared out the window. The wind had increased since she had arrived and the rain was pelting down. The sounds outside, even with the roar, where comforting as a bang on buckets and tins against the house roof. It was music of the natural kind that gave comfort to the soul. Her body felt the tingling of a woman in her youth, but she didn't want to give in to her feelings for Jake. She was afraid of the social stigma attached to it that came from her generation. She reckoned she would just get her clothes and head home in awhile, satisfied that soon she would wed this wonderful old man, who for reason she could not understand loved her with his all. She mulled all these things over as she sat and sipped her coffee.

"I'll be out in a minute, Sal," he said.

"Take your time, Jake, I'm in no hurry."

He took her things out of the dryer and hung them up, folding her undies in a careful manner as any man could do. He brought them around the corner for her and handed them to her sheepishly. "I'm sorry, I'm not very good at this," he said, "I haven't had very much practice."

She smiled at him. "It looks just fine to me, Jake. You took great care to do this for me and it's the loving act that you did that's more important than how they look."

"Why don't you spend the night with me, Sal? I could use your arms around me tonight, and I promise I won't touch you if you don't want me to."

"I'm not worried about you touching me, Jake. It just wouldn't look good," she said.

"Well, at least let me warm up your car. Okay? I don't want you to go out in this rain any more than you have to."

"Sure, Jake. I'll get dressed while you do that." She gathered up her clothes and put her cup in the sink.

Jake headed out the door and Sally went up the stairs and began to put on her clothes. When she had most of them on, she sat down at the vanity table. Combing her hair, she began to look at the lines in her face. *I'm getting so old,* she thought. *Why does Jake even bother with me? I only see it when I look in the mirror this age thing that has crept up on me. When I look at myself from the inside out, I feel and see the young girl I was of yesterday. Why do we have to grow old? Why the wrinkles? Where did the young girl go?* She let herself cry for the lost girl she longed for. An arm came around her, holding her gently and she looked up.

"Why are you crying, Sal?" he said, "Why are you so sad?"

"Oh," catching a sob in her throat, "just for the lost girl of yesterday and all the days before. I guess I'm not taking my age thing very well," she said as she looked away.

He took her face and gently turned her to the mirror and said, "Look at the beautiful woman I see looking back at me. I don't see any wrinkles; I don't see anything but beauty in this face here in the mirror. And you will never convince me she is anything else but beautiful."

"Jaaaake," she said, trying to turn her head away.

"No, Sal, now you listen to me. For every smile line you have on your face is time you have spent making others happy, regardless of how you feel. There is more beauty in your face than in someone who hasn't any lines. They haven't made a difference in anyone's lives but their own. They have been shallow all their lives, tuned only into themselves and their own feelings. They haven't time to do for others, or to be there for others. And when they complain, it's because something hasn't been done for them and they haven't gotten their way. When they die, Sal, shallow, and forgotten, they haven't even a clue how to touch someone else's life or where to begin to do God's work. I'm so very glad you are not like that. I'm glad you care and I don't see any lines in your beautiful face," he said as he wiped away her tears. "Besides, I love you more than anything and it hurts me when I see you cry."

"Jake," she said quietly.

"Yes, Sal," he replied, his hand caressing her face

"Thanks for that, I guess I needed to hear it from you. I have loved you a long time now, Jake. Don't ever believe otherwise."

"I won't," he said, smiling. "By the way, you have to spend the night with me anyway. Your old car gave up the ship and it won't start. Something to do with the starter, and I'm not going to get any more soaked than I am until morning and I can see better."

"You think it's my starter?" she asked.

"Yes, but I can't work on it in this. Besides, I may have to run into town in the morning and get a new starter from Napa. In the meantime, you're with me kid, and YOU," he said smiling, "don't have any choice."

"How do I know you didn't do this on purpose?" she said, smiling.

"You don't," he laughed. "You'll just have to wait and see, won't you, missy. Now you have two choices," he said, grinning. "You can sleep in here in the spare room and be safe from an old man, or you can come to my room and be cuddled all night and maybe get attacked by this same old man."

"HMMMMM choices, choices, choices," she said, smiling. "I think...I think..."

"Is it that hard to decide?" said Jake, laughing.

"Not at all." She smiled, put her arm around his waist and said, "Lead the way, you low life. You devil, you. You know, of course, this means you have to marry me after all, and soon. I'm going to be a wanton woman now."

"I know." He sighed. "Such burdens you women put on us men." He smiled and they walked arm and arm to his room and the door shut behind them, leaving them in a world of their own.

Chapter Fifty-Four

Jeff dreamed he heard bells ringing and they rang on and on. *Is the train coming?* He looked down the track. *There isn't a track.* The sound got louder, it felt like he was being crushed by the sound. Suddenly he jolted awake. It was his phone. He numbly felt for it on his night stand, for it was still dark and it was still raining, and there wasn't any light in his room.

"Hello?" he said, drowsy-like. "CHARLIE! What are you doing calling me at this hour? And what hour is it anyway. Four o'clock! Are you nuts, Charlie? This better be good, that's all I've got say for you. Okay, shoot."

As Charlie explained the why of his early morning call, Jeff suddenly sat up, reaching for his light and listening closely. "Are you sure?" he said, and it was a positive. "Yes, uhhuh, no, don't even breathe on anyone. Listen, wake up Judge Ford, I know he's crabby and cantankerous, but wake him up anyway. Use my name and give him the facts. Tell him to call me. I have a few others to add to what you have told me and if he has trouble believing you that we need a search warrant this morning, signed sealed and delivered have him give me a call. I don't believe that the suspect will be home. You know the funerals are today. Yes, at three. Say, you going to be there at the house for awhile? Well, I'd like you to call me back when you get the word from the judge. Okay. Thanks," he said.

This was more than Jeff had hoped for. It had cleared up some questions he had from last night and it narrowed it down to the one suspect he had in mind. The thought blew him away, as he had a liking, very much a liking for the suspect. The mess he had made reaching for his phone in the dark was laying on the floor. He started to pick up his things when he noticed muddy shoe prints next to his bed. The hair on the back of his neck stood up. *Someone has been in my room,* he thought, *in my house. I know I locked my doors and windows.* He picked up the phone and dialed Charlie again.

"Charlie? Yeah, well, guess what? Our little bird has been in my house. Yeah, that's right. There's shoe prints, muddy ones on my floor by my bed. Damn straight it gave me chills. I know. That close, anyway I'm not touching anything. Call the lab boys and send them over, will you. I know I could do it, but I want you here as soon as you get everything set up. Yes, thanks, I could use a cup. I'm not going to touch even the coffee pot. Thanks, Charlie, see you in a few," he said, hanging up the phone. Jeff reached over, sidestepping the prints on the floor and picked up his pants and slipped into them. He found last night's paper. He was too tired to read and sat back on his bed waiting for the knock on his door.

Chapter Fifty-Five

Jeff wasn't sure how to handle what he had to do next. After all, it had to do with friendship and it, this, hinged on how delicately he could manage it. He called out to the Gannon ranch only to get Sally on the phone, and this surprised him as he had never known her to be this open about her relationship with Jake. She was very cooperative, though, and told him her car was giving her a fit last night in the storm, so she stayed the night there. Jake, she said, was in town getting the part for the car and would be back shortly. No, she said Rich wasn't home. He had left in a hurry last night. It seems that he as worried about Bess Cramer, and he was sure she wasn't doing well at all. Sally shared with him the details of last night concerning Bess's possible suicide and what Rich had found.

"Would you like Jake to give you a call when he arrives?" she said.

"No, I'm just needing to get in touch with Rich," he told her. "I'll call out or send someone to pick him up."

"Well, if you plan to do that, I'll need to know," said Sally. "I don't want to leave her alone."

"Well, in that case, could you plan to go over anyway?" he told her, then he remembered she was without her car. "Tell you what I'll do, I'll send Charlie out to pick you up first and he can take you over with him. He can drop you off and get Rich at the same time."

Sally said, "That will be just fine, but could you tell me exactly what is going on?"

"Not really, not at the moment," he said. "You'll know more before the day is out, though. And thanks for her help."

When Jeff hung up the phone, he sat tapping on his desk with his pencil looking out his window at the gray morning dawn. The rain had managed to calm down to a drizzle, leaving everything in a depressed state. Charlie had managed to whip up the forensic boys. Jeff's place was swept for prints and the prints identified…the judge was madder then hops when Charlie first got him, but soon cooled off and issued the search warrant, wishing them good luck.

God, how Jeff hated this. *Why do people do things like this?* he thought. *This whole thing could have been avoided. If people would only just walk away from relationships. Why is it necessary to murder someone?* he thought. *Look who's talking, ole boy. You were willing to keep Sarah's secret and not tell a soul. You didn't want anyone to know you had your fling with Mary either. No less willing to cover it up. And on top of that, you thought about doing her in yourself. You are supposed to be the law. Now doesn't that just fry your taters. Now you have to corner a friend. He doesn't leave you very much room, does he?* he thought, shaking his head. *He really put you in a corner. And there isn't anything I can do to stop this from going forward, there isn't anything I can do to help him at this point. I guess I had better get on with it instead of sittin' here moping about all this. Someone has to do this, I guess better it be me then someone else.*

Jeff picked up his phone and punched Charlie's line. "Charlie can you come in here in a minute?" he asked.

"Sure," said Charlie, "I'll be right there."

Jeff began tapping with his pencil again. He thought, *This habit has got to go.* "Charlie, I have a job for you to do," he said as the old guy pulled up a chair. "I want you to go out to the Gannon Ranch and pick up Sally."

Charlie looked at him like he had lost his mind, "How does that figure?" he said.

"Well, let me finish. I need you to drop her off at the Cramer place and pick up Rich Gannon and bring him in here, if you will," he said, explaining to him why Rich was there.

"Sure, I can do that," he said.

"You know, Charlie, I'm going to miss you when you retire in a few days. You are the best detective I have here, and you are going to be hard to replace."

"Well, I appreciate that, Jeff. I'm going to miss being here. I have thought about getting my private license when I'm done."

"That might not be a bad idea," said Jeff. "We could always use you for consulting on the side."

"Well, I'd better go," he said. "We are short on time and we have a lot to do." He stood up and pushed his chair back.

"I'll have everything ready on this end, Charlie, so when you get back we can do this as smooth as possible."

"Okay, boss," he said, and shut the door quietly behind him.

Jeff sat in his chair for a few moments, then he got up and followed Charlie out. He motioned for Smith and Crane to come into his office. He shut the door behind them and began his conference with them. When he was done, he came out and poured himself a cup of coffee, taking it back to his office. He began to sift through the paperwork on his desk, making notes here and there to remind himself of the questions he wanted to ask.

It is a good thing, he thought, *that I have a secret drawer that no one knows about. Otherwise, my mouse would have gotten a hold of some mighty important papers.* He thought, *How could anyone have missed that piece of wood I keep there; I would have thought it would be obvious.* He shook his head. *Apparently not though, or the mouse wouldn't have left everything in a mess, fingerprints and the piece of wood out in the open that always slips out when someone is in my drawer. Won't wonders ever cease? Just two more hours,* he thought, *and I hope we have a confession. I'll be glad when my day is done and this is over.*

The rain had let up some in town and few streaks of sunshine were filtering through the clouds. They looked like angel wings touching the earth. The birds chirped here and there and the people of Lakeview milled about the town, carrying on with their lives as if nothing major was about to happen, that a murderer was about to be caught. Only thing that mattered in their lives was what might matter to anyone of them at all, and Jeff felt the weight of it bearing down on his shoulders.

Chapter Fifty-Six

Bess dreamed he held her in his arms. They were strong and loving. She felt his strength, and somehow knew things would be right again. Though her thoughts would return to the guilt she felt for stealing his heart away from his family, yet she felt so safe somehow and it confused her. It seemed in her mind he was close, but she couldn't get past the sleep state that her body was demanding of her. As fretful as it was, sleeping was all she could seem to manage at the moment. She thought she felt him leave her, but she wasn't sure. She tossed and turned and heard voices. Some were familiar, like Sally, and others were not. She wondered if she would ever get awake. Then she would drift off again, deep into the darkness that her body had provided for her, protecting her from the pain of the living world. Keeping her safe in time for the moment.

Sally closed the door behind Charlie and Rich, then looking around, she decided to throw on the fire another chunk of wood. The rain was at a drizzle and she felt a chill clear to the bone. Jake hadn't gotten back when she left the ranch, so she had written him a note letting him know where she was and what she knew for the moment. She knew he'd be over as soon as he had gotten the note.

Sally had brought her needles, so she sat and knitted by the fire. She had checked in on Bess before she began and had noticed that the girl was sleeping fretfully, but knew the more sleep she got the more her body and mind would heal. Sally heard the teakettle whistle and set her work down. She looked in Bess's cupboard for a cup and the tea bags. Finding both, she poured the steaming water into her cup. *I like her little house*, she thought, as she sat herself at the table. *Her kitchen is old but it has a warm feel to it. I wonder what the sheriff sent Charlie out here to get Rich for. Nothing much was said,* she thought. Charlie just said they had a few questions they needed to ask and so he was sent to pick up Rich. Don't worry yourself he had told her.

But it did worry Sally and she wished Jake would hurry up and get there. She didn't like being in the dark. She took her cup, and leaving the door open, she sat in the rocker in Bess's room and began to work on her afghan again. The rain tapped gently on the window, giving the house a peaceful feel to it, lulling Sally, and without realizing it she drifted off in the chair.

Chapter Fifty-Seven

When Jake got Sally's note, he didn't like the sound of it. He left the car part in the garage with the old car of hers and came straight away from the ranch. When he pulled up, he could see the smoke coming from the chimney.

Well, it looks like the ole gal has the fire going good, he thought. He knocked lightly, not wanting to wake Bess, but he got no response. He stepped quietly into the house and looked around. No sign of anyone. Then he went into the living room and saw the bedroom door was open. He grinned as he looked into the room and saw not only Bess asleep, but his bride to be as well. He decided for the moment not to disturb either of them and shut the door quietly. He picked up the phone and dialed the sheriff's office and ask for Jeff.

He spoke so quietly that the officer on the other end had to ask him to repeat what he said. "I said, can I speak to Jeff? I'm sure he is busy right now, but I want to speak to him now. Not tomorrow, not this afternoon, I mean now. Yes, it's important, and no, it's none of your damn business. Now get me Jeff," he demanded.

Jeff was not in the mood to take crap off of anyone and that included Jake. He didn't want to talk to him. *There isn't time, and besides,* he thought, *who does he think he is demanding my attention right now this very minute? Don't I have enough to do without all this garbage?* he thought.

"NO, I'm not talking to him right now! LUPE!" hollered the sheriff. "You tell him HE can wait. Tell him that I'm busy right now and I can't be disturbed." He saw Bob arrive through the door and he wanted to catch him before he got too far.

"Okay," she said, "will doooo."

Walking through the door, Bob asked Lupe what that was all about. She just shook her head and said the boss has been on a crank all morning long, she didn't really know why.

Bob looked in the door of Jeff's office and saw him motion for him to come in. He had Charlie in a chair and Rich was just leaving.

"Hi Bob," he said as he left the office. "How's your mom doing?"

"Just fine, Rich," he said. "As a matter of fact, I spent the morning with her. Winding Hills is a good rest home; they've taken real good care of her."

"Well, the next time you see her, tell her I said hi for me, will you?"

"Sure, thanks for asking. She'll appreciate that."

"Bob, come on in," said Jeff. "Shut the door behind you, will yuh? Sit down, I need to talk to you."

"Sure, what's this all about?" he said, looking at Charlie nervously.

"Well, for starters, Bob, I need your badge and gun," he said quietly.

"WHY? WHAT for? What's going on here?" he said.

Jeff walked around from behind his desk. Putting his hand on Bob's chair, he held open his hand to receive the gun and badge. "Bob, when good cops go bad, well, you make me sick to my stomach, son," he said.

Bob just looked at him, "I don't know what you mean."

"Yes, you do, boy. I really thought I knew you. I thought you would be our newest detective. How stupid do you think I am?" said Jeff.

"What's this all about?" asked Bob, setting his gun and badge on the sheriff's desk.

"The night when Mary died in the hospital you were there," he said.

"Well, you were there too," said Bob.

"Yes, I was, but it was my job to be there. Besides, we didn't find my prints on the murder weapon, only yours."

"I went in to see Mary; she was a close personal friend of mine, you know."

"Okay. I'll grant you that, but why were your prints on the syringe?"

"I don't know—I could have touched anything in her room," he said.

"Well, I might have accepted that, but here's the problem. The nurses don't open the syringes until they get into the room. The needles are kept sterile and sealed until used...we found your prints in Sarah's room too, and on the door, walls and glass in the meds room. How do you explain that?"

"I went in to see Sarah. Do you have a problem with that? She was asleep, so I didn't stay. And you know that night was crazy. I really don't know why they showed up in the medication room. I could have been talking to one of the nurses, who knows?"

"Well, while you are explaining things, answer me this. You have never been in my house that I know of, have you?"

"One time was there, I delivered papers on the Olsen case for you."

"SHIT, BOB, that doesn't get it with me. That was well over two years ago and, besides, your shoe prints were found next to my bed, you little pecker head. You pilfered through my things and left my stuff a mess!"

"What makes you think the shoe prints were mine," he said, squirming in his chair.

"We had a warrant and went into your house this morning, Bob, and we found your muddy shoes and they match exactly."

"I don't give a damn what you did or what you think you found, Jeff. It still doesn't prove I killed Mary."

"Yeah, well, it gets worse for you, Bob. Your prints were found in this office this morning and on my desk."

Bob started laughing, "Hey my prints are always in here. I work here, you idiot, where do you think they would be?" he said, smiling. "That doesn't prove a damn thing."

"Wipe that smile off your face, you little son of a bitch," Jeff said, getting red in the face. "Let me tell you something, you little asshole," he said. "I wiped everything clean last night when I left, and I purposely locked everything up. When you broke in, you forgot to relock my desk. Did you know that it has a piece of wood that comes loose when you get into it?"

"Maybe you didn't get it as clean as you thought," he said.

Charlie just shook his head. "Bob, you might as well come clean. We have you dead to rights. You know that little trip I took? Well, it wasn't vacation time after all. I spent my time driving to all the towns surrounding here looking for the jeweler who made that special of the bracelet that Mary wore. You know, Bob, the back of that bracelet had the initials B.T.J and the words I love you. Those initials are the exact match to your name. So I included your face with all the other photos. I must have walked a million miles and talked to about just that many people."

"Anyone could have those same initials and you know it," he said.

"Well, that's possible, you know, but not probable. Do you know what I found out while I was there?"

"Yeah, tell me, smart-ass! What DID you find out?" he said, smirking.

"Well, when I got to the big city of Bend, the jeweler there in a small shop downtown identified not only the bracelet, but he picked out your picture among five others."

"I don't believe it. You don't have that bracelet. You're just bluffing," he said.

"Why, because you stole it from the evidence room?" said Charlie. "You know Chuck called us and said it was missing. It had to be either you or me.

It wasn't me. I only took pictures when I saw it, so that leaves you, buddy," he said, setting it down on the sheriff's desk.

"Where'd you get that?" asked Bob.

"Remember that search warrant? Well, we found it along with the shoes."

"Okay! So I took it. I gave it to Mary a long time ago and I wanted to keep it as a memento of our friendship. You know how it is. That still doesn't prove anything, it's all circumstantial and you know it. This is pure bullshit."

"A witness called us and said they had seen you following Mary on four different occasions, and another one across from the Essex said you were sitting outside the motel where Mary Gannon and Juan Lopez had gone in. They thought you were on surveillance. You were, buddy, but not for us."

"You still don't have a God damn thing," he said, "Now either book me, and read me my rights, and get me a lawyer, or let me go."

"Well, if that's what you want," said Jeff. "But I have one more little thing I want to talk to you about. As you know, we had Rich in this morning and he hadn't been with Mary for a long, long time. Bob, did you know Mary was pregnant when she died?"

"Bullshit," he snapped. "She said she got rid, oh my God," he said as he raised his head back. "Oh my God!" and it broke him. He slumped in his chair and sobbed. "Oh my God." And he put his hands over his face. "Oh my God, I didn't know. I'm so sorry."

Jeff looked at Charlie and Charlie shrugged his shoulders like, "Hey, don't ask me I don't know."

Jeff decided to ask him, "Was it your baby, Bob?"

Bob just nodded his head yes.

"Did she tell you she got rid of it?"

"Yes, she did," he said, looking away. "If you want, I'll tell you everything now," he said quietly.

"Do you want a lawyer?" asked Charlie.

"No," said Bob.

"I'm going to have to read you your rights, Bob, and maybe you shouldn't say anything more until we can get someone to represent you."

"No, I want to get this off my chest if it's all right with you."

"Sure, Bob," said Jeff quietly, "sure," and he patted his back gently. He picked up pad and pen and slid them over to Bob. "I need you to write everything down on this paper and date it and sign it when you're done. Okay?"

"Sure, Jeff. No problem," he said weakly, reaching for the paper.

Chapter Fifty-Eight

Lupe had been watching them through the window for over an hour now and her curiosity was getting the best of her. It seemed to her that they were arguing some and that Charlie and the sheriff were teaming up against Bob. Bob looked nervous. He was fidgeting and finally he broke down and cried. That's when the sheriff shut the shades on the window. He looked Lupe straight in the eye. This made her a bit nervous as she got caught gawking and that is not what she wanted. Lupe had worked hard for her position and the respect she got in this office. She didn't want to jeopardize it now. Just as she was thinking this, the sheriff was standing at her desk and he handed her his papers.

"I want you to type these up for me if you will. I, ah, well, Lupe, I trust you to do this for me and file them in the proper place, and Lupe, when you read these…"

"Yes, Sheriff?" she said.

"Well just keep it to yourself, at least for now. We'll be booking Bob."

"Huh?" she gasped.

"Yes, and he's going to have a lawyer popping in here any minute. I just don't want to discuss it right now, Lupe. It's self-explanatory, it says it all in the confession I just handed you, okay?"

"Sure, Sheriff," she said, and Lupe began to read.

I knew Mary long before she even met Rich and that was a long time ago. I guess you could say I fell in love with her the moment my eyes lit on her. She liked the hard and fast lane in life and maybe that was what drew me to her. She was beautiful and she knew it. Oh, I knew she like to screw all the men, she never made any bones about it. But when she was with me it felt like I was the only one in the world. I guess you could say I was hooked, it made me feel like I was the only one. I don't know if that was bad or good. Then she set her sights on Rich. She told me she was planning to marry him the minute she saw him just because he was so unattainable. She planned to pretend she was pregnant, but it backfired on her and she did get knocked up. Well, hell, I figured she would have an abortion, but not Mary. You couldn't out guess her, so Tylor was born. She had decided the baby was good insurance, besides, she was after bigger fish. She wanted the Gannon ranch.

She didn't want to depend on her folks giving her money, as she had overheard them talking about making her try the world out on her own one day without their money. She didn't cotton to that idea. I wanted to marry her right then. I told her to divorce Rich, I would take care of her, but she laughed at me and said, "Honey, I don't know if you will ever have enough money to make me happy." Anyway, the next thing I knew she was pregnant again...only this time it was with Kaileen.

Well, then she said she got fixed when she was born and like a stupid fool I believed her. I picked her up that day that her and Rich had their fight...at first I thought he had beat the crap out of her, and I was mad. I figured I'd pick him up on a warrant or somethin'. But she told me hold on to your horses. As bad as that was, good in her eyes, and while he had hit her he had said he was sorry and he would never touch another woman again. She was glad he had cooled off like that cause it gave her time to come up with a better plan. She explained to me then that he had left to go out to the fields and then that is when she had cut her finger on a knife in the kitchen trying to get out ice from the tray. She said, "Leave him alone, Bob. I have bigger plans for him, he will pay for this some other way." She said, "I'm hoping they will think he murdered me and buried me somewhere." Well, I took her home with me and she was with me for about three weeks when we decided it might be better if she stayed with Sarah. I knew how strong Rich is, and I didn't really want to tangle with him.

All this was fine and good except that Mary calls me one day and says she pregnant and with my child. I'm excited, you see, as I've never been a dad before, only before I can get thrilled about this, she informs me she's going to get rid of it that she didn't want any more brats. I can't tell you how that made me feel. It was like a kick in the gut. Like the worst feeling I have ever felt. I begged her to reconsider, said I would raise my child. I even broke down and cried, it sickened me. I told her I thought she got fixed when Kaileen was born? No she said, she just had said that. But now she wasn't going to fool around about it. She was going to have it taken care of, along with getting rid of the kid. She told me she needed money for both and I had better come up with it, as she had run out of the twelve-thousand dollars that she had taken from Rich's account. I went to my uncle and I told him I was in trouble big time, didn't tell him what for, but that I needed money and fast. He loaned me eight-thousand dollars without blinking an eye. I gave this to Mary and drove her to the abortion center in Salem, Oregon. She said she didn't want me there. I was not to stay and wait for her. No, she said she would find a way back. I didn't know what to do at this point, but again I begged her to give me the chance to be a dad. I told her how much it would mean to me. I even reminded her that we had gone back a long ways and that I had always loved her. She told me it just wasn't in the cards, Bobby, she said. She always called me Bobby, especially when she wanted her way. It didn't do me any good. It tore me up inside anyway, like nothing I ever have felt in my life.

I believed that day she had gotten rid of my baby and she never did tell me how she got back home here. I left her there not knowing for sure if she had gone through the doors of that center or not. The next thing I knew she was at Sarah's place and staying with her. I knew she would surface before Rich would get into very much trouble, because as fast as she had gone through that money she had stole from the ranch account she would soon be in need of more money and I also knew our forensic team would justify all the blood at his place and that he would be cleared. Then when Mary decided to come back to life after our big snowstorm, she began strutting around town like nothing had ever happened. I tried to talk to her, but she didn't want a whole lot to do with me, though she did meet with me a couple of times. When she found out about how Rich almost died in that big storm, she said she wished he had died, that her plans were to get his place and all his money. And on top of that, Mary hated Jake anyway and I knew why. The old man had turned her down when she approached him sexually and that pissed her off. She said no one turns the great Mary down. She had plans in the works to get rid of him and off that place too.

I started to realize how much poison was in that girl. Yes, I was watching her and following her, and she didn't even know it. I just didn't realize that people were watching me. The night of Mary's accident it was a real mess in here at the hospital. It gave me the opportunity to listen in on the conversation between Sarah and Jeff, and when Jeff left the room I did as well. When I heard how much more pain she was causing, I decided it was time to let her go, out of this world and into the next.

I walked down the hall to the medication room and found all that I needed. It was easy to lift the morphine bottle out of the meds room as everyone was rushing around panicking. Some of the doctors were screaming at the nurses and nurses were hollering at the orderlies and it was one big mess. No one *knew what was going on and one of the nurses had left the door unlocked in her rush after she got her ass chewed by the doc. No one noticed a cop wandering the halls. Hell, I was a part of the normal make up of the place. No one saw me, as it was a mess with the Cramer girl and Sarah and Mary. I waited until the hospital settled down and everyone was exhausted in the wee hours of the morning and then I went into Mary's room. I looked at her all battered, and I felt sick because I knew what I was about to do. I loved her so, and it wasn't easy knowing what I had to do. I filled the syringe and I put it in the shunt in her arm and squeezed it all in, taking the life of this bad seed on earth. I cried as I left. It hurt like hell. I never loved anyone like I love that girl. I knew I would miss her and that my life would be empty without her.*

Then I quietly left the hospital unseen. I thought. Well, I don't know what I thought; I guess maybe no one would know the difference. Somehow in my mind it never occurred to me that any of this would show up, that everyone would think she just died of the car accident. I wasn't thinking about getting caught or that what I did was wrong at the time. I only wanted to stop her, I wanted to stop the pain she was causing everyone around her. So, when the sheriff, or Jeff, started to investigate, I started to panic. That's when I broke into his home. I had gone to True Value and got duplicates of all his keys. It wasn't hard, you know, they just thought it was for the office and they didn't have any reason to question me. I paid cash and so they wouldn't get suspicious and I asked for a receipt. The same goes for the keys to Jeff's desk and office. I guess I got sloppy, 'cause I left a lot of real dumb mistakes behind though, other wise I never would have got caught.

Anyway, I didn't know she had kept my baby. I'm sorry. I'm so sorry.

Signed Bob T. Jons
5-3-02
Time 1:26 p.m.

Lupe set the papers down. She had a sickening feeling in her stomach. She thought back about all the questions Bob had been pumping away at her all this time, and now it all made sense to her. She wondered what would happen to him. Up until all this, he had been as straight as they come. She thought about the times they had worked together and how you never really know someone like you think you do. She shivered, not from cold, but from the reality of it all. Pulling herself from a dream-like state she began to get back to the business at hand. Popping the paper into her typewriter, she began to fill the pages. The office around her was bustling with noise, mostly oblivious to what just happened as the working day had only just begun for some. The door clicked behind the lawyer that had been summoned for Bob, and from here after it would seem forever strangely vacant in the room.

Chapter Fifty-Nine

Six months later…

The leaves on the trees were turning to gold, copper and brown, and for some this was the best time of year. The weather was cooler and the gusts of wind were warm as they beckoned for the leaves to scatter on the ground. The townspeople found healing in the new marriages of those in love and with time, though not forgotten they would not refer to themselves as the town that had that awful murder. Deanie loved on her grandchildren and paid no mind that they were not officially hers. For in her mind she owned the privilege of being their grandmother and no one had better dare say otherwise. She found healing through them and this was good. She reached out and was working hard to earn the right to be called mom from the daughter who was stolen from her at birth. She desperately missed Wesley, and it was more than she could bear sometimes, but she found solace in working the ranch and it brought peace to her heart.

The sheriff had quit his job. He didn't need the money and he felt he couldn't do justice to it if he had to question turning in the one he loved. It had been too much on him to send his friend Bob to prison, and he felt it best to move on in his life. Besides, Sam was now running for local sheriff and he hoped he would win. He helped him put up the signs and campaigned heavily for him. As soon as he saw his friend elected, he was leaving, heading out to explore the world. Sarah and Jeff had decided the stress of the trial was too much and they chose not marry. This had saddened them both, for the love was there, but it wasn't enough to keep them together.

Charlie retired with his good name intact. He was known as the five star detective and this made him smile. He had planned to stay in the town, but on vacation Charlie had run across an old friend and had found love in his late life and married. She was a good woman, and Charlie set up his agency in her town, the town of Catchberry. She became his wife, secretary, and researcher. He sold his old house to his friend Jesse and he had made it into his photo studio. The old house never looked better with fresh paint inside and out.

Charlie was no longer lonely and found he could open up and share things he had no idea were possible. He had found peace at last.

Ole Mex liked working for the Gannon ranch and he did such a good job, he and his wife found security, a home and a pension, as Rich offered all this in exchange for their hard work. He worked hard every day trying to prove to Rich that he had not made a bad decision. The home that was deeded to them felt like a mansion and he never stepped inside the door before he gave the sign of the cross and a silent prayer of thanks to God for giving him such a wonderful friend.

Lupe became second in command at the sheriff's office She had passed her test to become their first woman detective. Her scoring was one of the highest ever seen. She and Sam were dating, but they chose to take it slow for they concentrated only on the upcoming election as high priority.

Jake and Sally married in a quiet ceremony with only a judge present and a couple of witnesses. He asked Sally not to work anymore, as he had plenty of money and it wasn't necessary for her to work for a living. She willingly turned the keys over to the Granger girl and sold her the adjoining house. Jake found them a nice piece of ground to build on and was having a log home built for Sally. He would still work with Rich, only now they were partners in the ranch and he could let ole Mex take over his old jobs. This was a long time coming and he was going to enjoy this newfound freedom.

"What time is it?" Bess asked.

"Oh," Rich said as he pulled her into his arms, "a hair past a freckle. Why? Why do you ask?" he said, gently smiling.

"The sun is going down," she said, shivering.

"You're cold," he said, rubbing her arms. "Would you like your wrap?"

"Yes, please, if it's not any trouble."

He left her sitting on the porch, her arms wrapped around herself keeping the chill off of her skin. Walking into the house, it echoed, for most of the furniture was gone. Soon the place would be no more and a new one built in its spot. He reached the door of their bedroom and noticed lying on the bed open was the book, and beside it was her wrap. He reached for the wrap and his fingers trickled across the book as he spotted his name. He picked it up and began to read.

If you are reading this then you must know it was and is my intention for you to do so. I want you to know how happy you have made me. Every day I wake up next to you is a new beginning and I thank God for sending you. When you're near, my body trembles and I know this is right. Most people go through life never having known this kind of love, nor do they know their soul mate. How lucky can I be? Just the luckiest girl alive and you made it all happen. I love you so deeply...I will always be here and you can always find me, I don't plan on ever going away. Sometimes yes, Sometimes fate can come and step in, just sometimes.

He picked up the pen and began to write.

Yes my love sometimes, *sometimes people like myself can get real lucky in love. Because of your persistence and love, I have found more than I deserve. I felt this strange pull toward you from the first moment I met you, and like you, I knew it was real. Sometimes we don't have any choices over the ones we love or who we know, or how it will turn out, but sometimes, my darling, it's for the good and our sometimes is forever. And, well, I love you too.*

He set the book down and picked up her wrap and walked over to the radio and turned it on. She looked up at him as he stepped out the door and he reached down and helped her up. "Would you dance with me, Mrs. Gannon?" he said as he put the wrap on her shoulders.

"Mr. Gannon," she smiled, "I'm as big as a barrel."

"Our baby won't mind us taking a slow dance," he said, cuddling. He began nuzzling her ear and he whispered softly, "Besides, you're so beautiful, I can't resist you."

"And you're too kind, sir," she said as she flowed into his arms.

The sun glowed, reflecting light on the clouds, making them a bright orange. Up on the hill above them stood a doe and a buck looking down from the forest trees on the pair who were slow dancing to the soft music. The world would go on and not all things would be good for everyone. But just once in a while things can be just right you know...SOMETIMES the wind whispered. Just sometimes...

CPSIA information can be obtained at www.ICGtesting.com
Printed in the USA
BVOW01s1216060414

349692BV00001B/51/P